Rachael Thomas has always loved reading romance and is thrilled to be a Harlequin Presents author. She lives and works on a farm in Wales—a far cry from the glamour of a Harlequin Presents story—but that makes slipping into her characters' worlds all the more appealing. When she's not writing or working on the farm, she enjoys photography and visiting historical castles and grand houses. Visit her at rachaelthomas.co.uk.

Books by Rachael Thomas

Harlequin Presents

The Sheikh's Last Mistress
New Year at the Boss's Bidding
From One Night to Wife
Craving Her Enemy's Touch
Claimed by the Sheikh
A Deal Before the Altar

Visit the Author Profile page at
Harlequin.com for more titles.

Dear Reader,

I was really excited to be part of The Billionaire's Legacy and with authors I've loved reading for a long time. In fact, it was an honor.

I fell in love with my hero, Liev, and really enjoyed writing his and Bianca's story, set against the backdrop of a city I have always wanted to visit. When I did, I was totally swept up by it and didn't want to leave.

I hope you enjoy meeting Liev and Bianca as much as I did.

Happy reading.

Rachael

Xx

This is dedicated to fellow members of
The Write Romantics:
Jo Bartlett, Sharon Booth, Jackie Ladbury,
Lynne Pardoe, Deirdre Palmer, Helen Phifer,
Jessica Redland, Helen J Rolfe and Alys West.
Thanks ladies for your friendship and support.

Before Bianca had time to respond he lowered his head, claimed her lips in a kiss that verged on demanding. Her head spun and although she knew she shouldn't, she moved her lips against his, tasting the forbidden. Her fingers clutched the lapels of Liev's jacket as he put his arms around her, pulling her close against him.

It was insane. It was also amazing.

"No." She pushed against him, and he pulled back but didn't let go of her. "That can never happen again, not like that."

Liev drew in a deep breath and let it go slowly, as if curbing an angry response. "It will if we are in public. If it's part of your role, as you called it."

"Just go," she snapped, and relief and disappointment washed over her as he moved back from her. "Go, Liev. This charade is over for tonight."

"Until tomorrow, Bianca."

With those words haunting her Bianca watched him stride back to the elevator, wondering what had just happened. Why had she taunted him, but more important, why had she kissed him?

It would not happen again.

Rachael Thomas

TO BLACKMAIL A DI SIONE

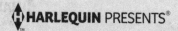

HARLEQUIN PRESENTS®

Recycling programs
for this product may
not exist in your area.

ISBN-13: 978-0-373-13940-8

To Blackmail a Di Sione

First North American publication 2016

Copyright © 2016 by Harlequin Books S.A.

Special thanks and acknowledgment are given to Rachael Thomas
for her contribution to The Billionaire's Legacy series.

HARLEQUIN®
www.Harlequin.com

Printed in U.S.A.

CHAPTER ONE

Bianca Di Sione scanned the busy conference room from her vantage point at the back, looking for her sister Allegra. The buzz of voices became louder as the room filled but she was too preoccupied to notice. She couldn't quite shake off the sensation that things weren't right with her sister. Not that she'd mentioned anything to her. That would be so unlike Allegra.

As the conference got under way, Bianca saw Allegra walking onto the stage and knew something was wrong. She was pale beneath the polished exterior she always showed to the world and Bianca felt guilty. She was about to add to that worry. The weight of their terminally ill grandfather's request would only exacerbate whatever worried Allegra, but she had to talk to her. She needed to confide in someone and Allegra had always been that person. She'd stepped into the role of mother after the tragic loss of their parents when they were young and had always been there for her.

The final speaker was introduced but Bianca couldn't concentrate; her mind kept replaying what her grandfather had asked of her last week. He'd been so frail, so weak, she hadn't wanted to press him for more information, but now wished she had. All she had to go on was the tale of his Lost Mistresses, which she and her brothers and sisters had grown up on. Even more intriguing, she wasn't the only grandchild to be sent on a mission to retrieve one of these Lost Mistresses, but she did understand how important they were to him. She recalled the many times he'd told them that these precious pieces were how he'd managed to set up Di Sione Shipping when he arrived in America. He'd *always* referred to them as their legacy.

'Ms Di Sione. This is an unexpected pleasure.'

That voice, that accent which hadn't quite had the roughened edges smoothed from it, startled her from her reverie. She turned and looked up into the hard but undeniably handsome face of Liev Dragunov.

He looked immaculate, his dark suit emphasising the hardness which sparked from his ice-grey eyes, his brown hair short and as severe as his expression. He looked formidable. Just as he had the first day she'd met him, when he'd approached her company to represent his. The firm line of his mouth hinted that a smile lingered just beneath the surface. Inwardly her heart plummeted. She didn't need this, not today. Couldn't the man take no for an answer?

'Mr Dragunov. I trust you are here for legitimate reasons.' The same unease she'd felt the very first time he'd stood in her office last week shivered down her spine. She even began to wonder if she was losing her ability to read a person. Allegra was being unusually evasive, probably due to all the travelling she'd done recently. But this man, with his commanding presence and dominating aura, unsettled her far too much.

'Everything I do has a legitimate reason.' Was that an undertone of threat in his accented voice?

She lifted a brow in speculation as she looked at him, not totally immune to his bad-boy looks. Her gaze slid discreetly over him as he surveyed the room. He pulled at the cuffs of his white shirt, visible beneath his dark suit, as if he was preparing himself for some kind of battle or confrontation. In response she found herself compelled to stand just a little taller, as if hoping to match his height.

'That may be so, but what possible reason could you have to be here, Mr Dragunov? Geneva is a long way from New York.' He turned his attention back to her and she looked directly into his eyes, resisting the urge to shiver at the coldness in them. Instead she kept her chin lifted and her face a mask of composure, hiding her unease, something she'd become more than adept at over the years.

'As I made a sizeable donation to the Di Sione Foundation, I think it is prudent to see what work is being done. Would you not agree, Ms Di Sione?' He moved a little closer to her, lowering his voice, and even though his polite smile didn't falter she sensed something more.

'Do you have an interest in creating opportunities for women in developing countries, Mr Dragunov?' Bianca couldn't keep the crispness from her voice. Neither did she miss the hardening of his jaw, or the glint of steel in his eyes. Could he really be using the Di Sione Foundation as a way of speaking to her again? She'd made it clear her company was not in a position to handle his next launch campaign, something he obviously had difficulty accepting.

She clutched her folder tighter against her chest, unsure what it was about this man that made her feel nervous and also excited. He'd unlocked something inside her, provoked her in a way no other man had, and her instant response was to defend herself. But against what?

Already it was a sparring of words, just as it had been the first time he'd arrived in her office. She'd put her reaction to him down to shock of her grandfather's request, but wasn't so sure any more. Liev Dragunov was a force to be reckoned with and right now that was the last thing she wanted to do.

He didn't take his eyes off her but she refused to look away, refused to give him even one tiny amount of power over her. She'd learnt that trick early on in life—how to outwardly remain in control when inside she was all nerves and apprehension. It was many years since a man had made her feel so uneasy, but it had never been quite like this. Not that she'd ever allow the Russian billionaire to know that, not when he brought out her insecurities and vulnerabilities with just one glacial look.

'No. But I do have an interest in you.' The answer was blatant and she almost let a shocked gasp slip out but managed to hold it back.

Only once before had a man been so bold

about his interest in her and she'd almost fallen for it. Ten years on, the humiliation of her prom night still raced through her. Brought into the present by a man she instinctively didn't trust, yet was drawn to, like a moth to an irresistible flame.

What was it about him? Well, there was no way she would be finding out. Life was far too busy at the moment to indulge in such nonsense.

'I explained last week, Mr Dragunov, that I am not in a position to represent you or your company.' Irritation caused her words to be sharp and unyielding and his eyes narrowed slightly in suspicion, adding to his aura of power.

'I don't believe that.' He moved a step closer and she caught a hint of his aftershave, as strong and dominating as the man himself.

She couldn't look away, her gaze locking with his. Her pulse leapt and she wondered if she'd ever breathe normally again. Just when she thought she couldn't keep up the pretence of indifference any longer he stepped back.

'And I don't believe you do.' He continued before she could gather herself and form a reply. He looked back out across the room as he spoke, giving her much-needed time for recovery. When he turned his attention to her once more she was ready for him. 'You don't believe it at all.'

He really was pushing her too far and she glared at him, wondering if she should summon security. Then she recalled what he said, that he'd made a sizeable donation to the charity. Her sister's charity. She couldn't very well have him thrown out.

Allegra had enough worries at the moment and she couldn't heap on more, just because of a man who didn't understand no. She would have to deal with this herself. There was no way she could run a PR campaign for his company when it was a competitor of her biggest client. Couldn't he understand that?

'I meant what I said, Mr Dragunov.' She stayed behind the protective mask of professionalism she always wore, even though inside, things she'd long ago locked away were now being disturbed, just by his very presence. 'I am not in a position to discuss this now, but you are welcome to make an appointment with my secretary on your return to New York.'

Applause filled the room and she forced her attention to the stage, but she couldn't shake the feeling that he still had power over her.

Somehow he'd gained the advantage; she had no idea how, but he was now in a position above her and able to use that power. 'If you will excuse me, I need to speak with my sister,' she said quickly, grasping at the first thing she could think of. She hadn't felt this out of her depth for many years.

He looked at her, his hard gaze piercing into her soul, as if he could see everything she'd ever run from. She didn't like it, not one bit. There were enough worries on her mind without Liev Dragunov and his persistence adding to them.

'Have dinner with me tonight, Ms Di Sione. If after that you still do not want to represent my company, then I shall leave you in peace.'

Dinner? With this man? Why did the idea of sitting at a table over a glass of wine and dinner set her pulse racing so wildly?

'My answer will still be the same.' She kept her air of indifference, desperate to hide the rush of strange emotions which were now flowing through her. She hadn't had dinner with a man for a long time.

'Then nothing will be lost and we will have had the pleasure of one another's company.' A hint of a smile played on his lips and she wondered how he would look if he really smiled.

Would that hard expression soften? If it did, he'd melt every female heart in the vicinity.

'If I agree,' she began, not knowing where the words were coming from or why she was playing with fire in such a reckless way, 'you will find you have had a wasted evening, Mr Dragunov.'

'That is a chance I'm prepared to take.' He smiled at her, confirming her suspicions. He was lethal and already she could feel the innocent woman within her stirring, imagining things that would never be possible. Not with this man.

'What I'm saying, Mr Dragunov, is that I will not, under any circumstances, change my mind.'

'Just dinner, then? You are staying at this hotel, are you not?' He glanced at his watch and she found herself studying his strong hands, blushing slightly as he looked back at her.

'Yes, I am.' Suspicion raced through her. He seemed to know just a little too much about her, but she dismissed the idea as far-fetched, deciding she would uncover the reasons for his persistence.

'I will meet you in the lounge at seven-thirty.' His clipped tones, made harsh by his accent, brooked no argument, but she wasn't about to allow him to dominate her. If he still wanted her company to represent his, he had to realise she called the shots.

'I'm not sure it's such a good idea.' Bianca remained forceful, keeping her words strong. He was like no other man she'd met; he was indomitable, but there was something else. When he'd left her office she'd made her usual client searches, but nothing had shown up. No reason to refuse his business other than the fact that he was a potential competitor of her brother's company, ICE.

'A business dinner, Ms Di Sione.' The broad width of his shoulders rose as he drew in a deep breath, the only hint that he was working at keeping up the cool aloofness which almost dripped from him. 'It is still my hope that I can persuade you to represent my company.'

'That isn't possible,' she began, but to her disbelief he cut her off midsentence.

'Just dinner.'

Liev watched Bianca Di Sione look around the room as the speaker finished to a rapturous applause. He couldn't help a smile of satisfaction. Finally, he'd begun to crack the ice princess. His previous attempts, all businesslike and professional, had missed their target, but it seemed that, like most women and one in particular from his past, fine wine and candlelight dining were all that was required. The auction brochure on Bianca's desk last week had given him that clue; if sparkling jewels caught her attention, then so would dinner, even if it was offered and accepted under the guise of a business meal.

As they'd spoken he'd had to fight off the image of Bianca, long dark hair flowing freely around her shoulders as she sat opposite him at dinner, candles glowing, highlighting her beauty. The image filled his mind and fired his body with heat. No, he couldn't allow anything to threaten his plans. Even an attractive woman…and he knew well enough just how distracting and destructive a beautiful woman could be.

He'd slammed the door shut on such thoughts, pushing them roughly from his mind. Physically wanting the haughty Bianca Di Sione was not part of his plan. His strategy was to ensure her company represented his, allowing him to get closer to his ultimate goal. She was a necessary means to an end. Nothing more.

'Just dinner.' She glanced at her watch, then echoed his thoughts. 'Nothing more.'

'You have my word.'

She looked back at him and frowned. Briefly he caught a glimpse of vulnerability in the blue of her eyes as they met his, but then the glittering of icicles in hers froze him out. 'Why should I trust you? I don't know anything about you, Mr Dragunov. For a man with such a successful company, it is hard to find any information about you.'

So she had been researching him. She might have turned down the very generous amount he'd offered for her company to represent his, but she had still been interested enough to find out more. As always, money talked. 'I think you will find, the same can be said of yourself, Ms Di Sione.'

He knew all the ways to keep information under the radar, away from prying eyes, and from the subtle way she ran her company, it was a skill she, too, possessed.

'Which means, you have tried to find out more about me? Just as I have, about you.' This time there was a hint of amusement in her voice, the slightest curve of her lips. What would it be like to kiss them, to feel them soften beneath his? He erased the thought from his mind quickly, annoyed this fiery woman was getting to him.

'Isn't that what business is all about? Knowing who your enemies are?' He certainly knew who his enemies were. He'd known since he was just twelve years old, since his parents had died within months of each other. After the loss of the family business and home, he'd had to watch his father spiral into drunken oblivion, too depressed to care how sick his wife had become. Liev had been powerless to help and found himself alone with nowhere but the streets to live, forced to steal just to survive.

Those memories were etched in his mind, the scars going deep. The rage his father had shown, shocking him and his mother. The happy family they had once been, with the bright and prosperous future, was snatched away as even before his parents' deaths he'd had to fend for himself, his mother too sick and his father too intoxicated.

Oh, yes, he knew who his enemy was.

He doubted she had any idea what an enemy was, having grown up cosseted and protected from the big bad world by her family name. She would have wanted for nothing, would have had every luxury possible. The only thing in common they shared was the loss of their parents. Other than that they were worlds apart.

'Enemies?' Her eyes widened, the true extent of their blue showing clearly. 'Is that what we are?'

He looked at her, irritated he'd forgotten himself and spoken the truth. 'How could any man make an enemy of such a beautiful woman as you?'

To his amazement, she laughed, a soft gentle sound, which nudged at memories of happiness from long ago. 'Now you have gone too far, Mr Dragunov.' Her words were stern, but her smile lit up her face and the cold mask she hid behind slipped briefly away, revealing a very beautiful and alluring woman.

'Until this evening, Ms Di Sione.'

Before he could say anything else, or allow her to hypnotise him into forgetting precisely what he wanted, he left, assured that by the end of the evening she would be running a very prestigious and lucrative campaign for his company. His first step towards revenge against the company which had destroyed his parents would finally be under way.

'Are you sure you are quite well?' Bianca asked Allegra as her sister almost flopped down into a chair of the members' lounge with exhaustion. The conference had been a huge success, but she'd never seen her sister look so tired. She would normally be on a high after such an evening.

Grandfather's illness was obviously taking its toll, or rather his almost insistent requests that the treasures, his Lost Mistresses, be found. It had been a shock to discover that Matteo, her older brother, had also been asked to find one. As children they'd listened to Grandfather's tales of the precious trinkets he'd been forced to sell when he'd first arrived in America, but they didn't know the full story. Like Allegra and Matteo, she intended to do all she could to reunite Grandfather with the bracelet he'd told her of.

'Of course I am. Anyway, there are more important things to discuss, like who was that you were talking to earlier?'

'I was hoping you'd tell me as he's one of your biggest sponsors.' Bianca, still concerned at the paleness of Allegra's face, poured them both a glass of wine, a little alarmed when even that didn't interest her. 'He's a Russian billionaire who wants me to represent his company. He's quite insistent about it. A little too much, to be honest. If I didn't know any better, I'd say he's made a sizeable donation to the charity just to follow me here.'

Allegra's gaze met hers. 'And the problem with that is?'

'To start with, I'm representing ICE and Liev Dragunov is a competitor. But there's something else. I'm not sure what. There's just something about him.' It was something wild, as if life hadn't yet tamed him. Bianca was shocked by her thoughts, irritated he'd slipped inside her mind so easily.

'Other than his good looks?' Allegra teased. 'You really shouldn't shut every handsome man out of your life, Bianca. What happened with Dominic was ten years ago.'

'Then you will be pleased to know I have agreed to have dinner with him—to discuss representing his company, that is.'

'I see.' Allegra smiled and Bianca was relieved to see she looked more herself. It still didn't mean she could burden her with too much worry over their grandfather. Once they were back in New York there would be time to talk properly.

Bianca shook her head in mock reprisal. 'Don't, Allegra. I guess I'm preoccupied with Grandfather's failing health and his latest request. He's talked of the Lost Mistresses so often over the years they've become part of our childhood. I wonder why they are so important now.'

'I don't know, but Matteo's necklace and my Fabergé box don't seem connected in any way. How did Grandfather ever manage to have such priceless objects? He was so pleased to see the box, caressing it as if it really was a lost mistress.'

'I've had people looking into the whereabouts of the bracelet and it's coming up for auction in New York next week.' Bianca remembered the elation she'd felt at tracking down the bracelet. 'I did approach the owner and offered to buy it privately, but they were adamant as it was such a unique piece it would go to auction.'

'At least it will be easy for you to get. You will only need to bid for it,' Allegra said quickly, and again Bianca was curious about her sister's time in Dar-Aman, where the Fabergé box had been found.

'None of this makes any sense,' Bianca said, wondering if she should question Allegra further. 'But if it makes Grandfather smile whilst he is so ill, then I'll do anything for that.'

'Hadn't you better go?' Allegra looked at her watch, ever the mother figure. Or was her sister evading the questions which she longed to ask her?

Doubts began to creep into Bianca's mind about having agreed to dinner with Liev Dragunov. She had no intention of representing his company, and the fact that he was so persistent made her uneasy. There was something about him, something she couldn't quite pin down, and it was just one more thing to worry about that she really didn't need.

'Yes, I suppose I'd better not keep such a wealthy and persistent man waiting.'

By the time Bianca arrived at the bar that was exactly what she had done. She spotted him immediately. He stood out from all other men around him, not just because of his height and undeniable good looks. Even among other wealthy businessmen he had a commanding presence which dominated the room.

He was sat at the bar, his back to her as she walked up to him, which gave her time to take in his broad shoulders and the way his suit jacket fitted with perfection, emphasising strength without showing what she knew would be a body envied by men and admired by women.

His short brown hair, which she guessed had lightened in the sun, gave him a hardness she was convinced lurked beneath the surface of his show of wealth. There was no mistaking this man's success, displayed with tailored suits to expensive watches.

There was also a rawness about him which hinted at danger and was probably exactly what he exploited to attract women. But not her. She wasn't going to fall for that kind of destructive charm—not again.

'Sorry I'm a little late.' He turned as she spoke, his gaze sliding down the classic little black dress she'd chosen to wear. It was dressed up enough to go out to dinner in, but not so daring that it would give him any wrong ideas. If there was one man she needed to make herself clear to, it was Liev Dragunov.

She slipped onto the tall stool at the bar where he sat and made the mistake of looking directly into his eyes. These grey eyes held hints of blue, like the ocean as the spring sunshine finally danced on its surface after winter. They also appeared to be assessing her with calculated coolness.

'Isn't that a trait all women have?' The deep tones of his voice were courteous yet patronising, instantly putting her on the defensive.

'No. As it happens, it is not. I was detained with family matters. For which I apologise.'

'I took the liberty of ordering champagne.' He signalled to the bartender and a bottle of champagne was opened and poured into tall flutes before she could state her objection.

'You seem to be living under a lot of misconceptions as far as women are concerned, Mr Dragunov.'

He lifted his flute, his eyes challenging her to refuse his toast, but something sparked to life within her. Something that enjoyed the thought of the challenge Liev Dragunov represented. She chinked her flute against his, not able to suppress the smile which threatened.

'And one in particular.' He took a sip of the bubbly liquid.

Bianca blushed as she realised her scrutiny had been noticed. She could feel the conversation sliding off course before it had even begun. He was talking to her as if they were on a date, and despite the lightness of her mood, that was something which needed changing. 'Maybe you can explain about your company and why you are so insistent mine should represent it, that you contrive to be here in Geneva, donating to my sister's charitable cause.'

He lifted his brows and a hint of amusement lingered at the corners of the firm line of his lips. 'So we do have something to celebrate. We are at last discussing business.'

That was exactly how it would stay. Without even knowing how, he had managed to distract her and that was something she couldn't allow. Not now. She had to be focused. All her attention had to be channelled into getting the bracelet for Grandfather and Dario's new product launch next month. Handsome Russians didn't feature in her game plan at all.

'Discussing business does not mean it's a foregone conclusion that my company will represent yours, Mr Dragunov.' He might be charm itself, but she still hadn't decided why she didn't trust him. Her gut instinct warned her away from him, that he was hiding something either about himself or his company.

'I believe you have represented ICE.' His gunmetal-grey eyes darkened as his expression turned serious.

'Yes, that is correct.' She wasn't about to divulge that she still represented the company, that at this very moment she was in the middle of planning a launch for their latest product, or that ICE was headed by her brother Dario. 'And do you see your company as competition for ICE?'

'Would it be a problem if it was?' He leant

back in his seat and regarded her with what she could only describe as suspicion.

'It would certainly be a conflict of interests, Mr Dragunov. You must know, as you seemed to have researched my company very meticulously, that by representing ICE, I represent my brother Dario?'

Liev didn't outwardly flinch when she mentioned Dario Di Sione, owner of ICE and his first target for revenge, as he worked his way to the top. To do so would be to show his hand, and like any good gambler, he played his cards close to his chest.

'My company manufactures hardware and software that would complement ICE. We would not be in direct competition.' She looked directly at him and for a moment he thought he sensed her hesitation.

'Mr Dragunov,' she began, her voice firm, her chin held high, 'I represent ICE. The leader in the market. I cannot see any reason why I should jeopardise such a contract to represent your company—direct competitors or not.'

He clenched his jaw at her slight of his company, her rejection of him as a businessman. He may not be the market leader—yet—but the businessman he now was certainly wasn't accustomed to being spoken down to. He wouldn't even have tolerated it when he began rebuilding his father's business from the scraps that ICE's cruel takeover had left behind and he certainly wouldn't stand for it now.

'Would it help if I met you at your office with samples of the products? The following Wednesday, perhaps?'

'No. I'm sorry, Mr Dragunov. It wouldn't make any difference, and besides, I have an auction to attend the following Wednesday.' She stood up, picked up her purse, bringing their business dinner to a close before it had even begun.

Liev recalled the brochure he'd seen on her desk when he'd first visited her office and the mark against the bracelet. The ice queen had a passion for jewellery, confirming his first impression of her—a spoilt little rich girl, cut from the same cloth as the woman he'd once thought he wanted to marry.

'Very well, Ms Di Sione. You have made your feelings clear.' His terse tone had little effect on this cold woman. He looked at Bianca, pushing aside the flicker of interest he had in her as a woman, remembering his reason for seeking her out. His plan to find out all he needed to know of ICE may have been thwarted by her refusal to represent his company, but he was far from finished with her.

She was the key to the door of revenge on a company who had destroyed his parents and robbed him of his childhood, taking everything from him, including his freedom. There was more than one way to get what he wanted and she had just offered him an alternative. He would take something she treasured and desired, and now he knew exactly what that was.

CHAPTER TWO

THE AUCTION HAMMER BANGED, jangling Bianca's usually steady nerves. Just two more items and then the bracelet her grandfather had revealed to be one of the Lost Mistresses, and had asked her to find, was up.

She looked at the brochure image of emeralds and diamonds encrusted on delicate silver strands woven into the most beautiful bracelet. Never had his story conjured up the idea of such a priceless piece, one that would undoubtedly push her to her limits.

Annoyance that the present owners had turned down her more-than-generous offer to buy before it went to auction bubbled up again. They'd told her they had been reliably informed they stood to gain substantially more at auction. She'd raised her offer, but to no avail.

She refocused her attention as the auctioneer's voice penetrated her thoughts. Whatever happened now she had to hold her nerve; this was one bid she was going to win. She'd promised Grandfather she would do whatever she could to find the bracelet, and now that she had, there was no way she was going to let him down.

She took a deep breath as the hammer came down again and the gentle hum of speculative voices filled the room as the bidding on a gold brooch was completed. Movement at the side of the room caught her attention and, as she looked, every nerve in her body tingled with something akin to fear.

Liev Dragunov. What was he doing here? She'd already politely and professionally refused to represent his company. Not just because it would create a conflict of interest with Dario's new launch, but because he set off alarm bells in her head. He had such an unmistakeable aura of power about him and had continually proved that he didn't take no for an answer.

Why he was here at the auction of some of the finest jewels wasn't worth thinking about right now. She wasn't going to let him distract her, not when she was so close to getting the bracelet. Her grandfather's happiness rested on winning the next bid, and as public bidding and jewellery shopping were not one of her most favoured pastimes, she needed to concentrate. There would be time enough later to deal with Mr Dragunov's persistence—once and for all.

She smarted with indignation as he had the audacity to look over at her and smile, as if they were old friends. But she wasn't fooled. Even from this distance she could see that the smile hadn't reached those icy grey eyes and her feelings of mistrust deepened. Just what was he up to?

The hammer banged down again and she drew in a sharp breath of shock. Damn him. He'd almost distracted her, almost made her miss the bid. She focused her attention on the auctioneer, determination rising up from within. She would get this bracelet, no matter what.

'The next item, a stunning piece of craftsmanship, is a silver bracelet set with diamonds and emeralds.' The crisp voice of the immaculately suited auctioneer almost sliced through her nerves. She kept her focus on the wooden stand on which the auctioneer leant, looking out at the serious bidders in the audience.

The bidding started and subtly she nodded her bid, alarmed to see the price rising rapidly.

Not that it mattered. Her company was one of the most successful in her field; she didn't need to panic just yet, although she had to have this piece. Thankfully the bidding slowed and she breathed a sigh of relief as her bid remained the highest.

Just as the hammer was about to fall, the crowd gasped as a new and outrageously high bid was entered, pushing the price far too close to her top limit. She wanted to look around the room. See who it was who was denying her grandfather of one of his final requests, but in true Bianca style, she remained devoid of emotion and totally focused on the task.

As her heart thumped anxiously in her chest, she increased her bid, satisfied it was enough to dissuade even the most avid collector.

The crowd gasped again as the figures displayed on the screen rose steeply. Who was doing this to her? She bid again and glanced around the room, unable to locate the bidder. Then she saw Liev Dragunov nod at the auctioneer, outbidding her once again by a ridiculous amount. What was he doing?

Anger fizzed around her and all rational thought left her mind. She had to have this bracelet. Nothing else mattered. She bid again— her final bid—and already beyond her planned limit. She glared a warning at Liev. His face remained as if sculpted from ice, barely acknowledging her. To her outrage he bid again, not with the customary nod of his head but with bold and heavily accented words. He'd doubled her bid. Doubled it!

She reeled in shock and for a second nothing else existed, until the bang of the auctioneer's hammer completed the sale—and her loss. Her failure. How could she have let that happen?

The applause which followed Liev's insultingly high bid finally quietened, but the thumping of her heart didn't. She couldn't even move. She'd failed her grandfather. Allegra had told her all she needed to do was bid and she hadn't even been able to do that. Not getting the bracelet had never entered her head. Much less that Liev Dragunov would outbid her.

When sense finally returned and she left her seat, the humiliation of the moment burning on her cheeks, Liev was nowhere to be seen. Settling his debts, no doubt.

Suspicion slipped uncomfortably into her mind. Had he bid for the bracelet to force her hand into representing his company? It was so far-fetched it was ridiculous, but there was only one way to find out.

Confront him.

* * *

Liev waited. His patience had served him well, as had the overheard snatch of conversation with her sister about the bracelet. Now he was finally about to get what he wanted. Bianca Di Sione dancing to his tune.

He stood outside the auction room and watched her leave, glancing around her. From the furious expression on her face, she was obviously looking for him, the person who had deprived her of her latest little trinket. Just like a woman to have her head turned by a piece of expensive and sparkling jewellery.

There was no need to pursue her now, to cajole her into agreeing to act for his company. His sources had done well. Her discreet enquiries about the bracelet, which had been scheduled for auction, had allowed him to move in swiftly, persuade the vendors that his interest was genuine and under no circumstances should they accept any offers before the auction, that whatever happened he would double the bid.

Now he'd proved his bank balance was worthy of New York society and up to such a bid, he wanted to put his name among the elite of the business world and he would do exactly that through Bianca Di Sione. He had her much-longed-for bracelet, the one she would do anything for, and was sure she would fall in line with his new request.

He no longer only needed her to represent his company to get the information for the revenge he so badly wanted. He now had much bigger plans. She'd stood in his way, slighting him and his business, and now she would pay for that. Not only would he use the Di Sione name to open the doors of society which had remained firmly closed to him—a self-made Russian—he would ensure the Di Sione family never forgot his name.

'How could you?' Bianca's furious tones alerted him to her presence, even if the zip of energy which rushed through him hadn't.

He turned to face her, anger glowing on her cheeks and sparking in her eyes. There was more yet, of that he was sure, and he stood silently against her anger.

'You are unbelievable. You've just done this to get at me, because I wouldn't represent your company. I knew you were trouble, knew you couldn't be trusted.' Her hissed tirade continued, attracting the attention of passers-by. The fury in her face and the exasperation in her stance brought a smile to his lips. She looked quite beautiful, stunningly passionate, with her eyes sparking so wildly that he wanted to kiss her into silent submission.

'I had no idea you wanted the bracelet quite so badly.' He raised his brows speculatively as he looked down at her, sure his smooth tone was as irritating as the fact he'd bought the bracelet, belittling her as much as she had him in the bar in Geneva when she'd refused to represent his company. He could feel the heat of her anger burning him.

'You saw me bidding. You as good as stole it from me.'

Now his anger matched hers, but whereas hers was red hot, his was ice cold. Nobody branded him a thief and got away with it. 'Think what you like of me, Ms Di Sione, but never call me a thief.'

Her accusation hurtled him back to the days of living rough on the streets of St Petersburg. And he clenched his hands into tight fists at his sides, determined not to allow her to push him to the limits of his control.

'I need that bracelet.' There was only the merest hint of desperation in her voice. Anyone else might not detect it, but with years spent on the streets, fending for himself, he'd become adept at such a skill.

'I'm sorry. Did I deprive you of your latest

little trinket?' A bad taste filled his mouth as he again thought of her, growing up with the life of a princess, while he, along with other unfortunates, had sometimes not eaten for days.

'Why do you even want it?' She glared at him, her voice lower and more controlled, but her anger was all there in her eyes to see. He snapped the door closed on his past, knowing it would only make him angry—and anger wouldn't help him now, only cool control was needed.

He waited calmly as she fixed him with those dark eyes, her breathing coming fast and hard, as if they'd just shared a kiss. The thought sent a rush of awareness around him, flooding his body with an undeniable need to know her much more intimately, to know how she kissed, how she liked to be held, but he pushed aside those heated ideas. He must be fired up by the exchange and the thought that now he had her where he wanted her. 'That is none of your concern.'

'I'll pay you double what you bid.'

Double? Did she really want the piece that much? He already knew she was a woman who was easily distracted by such fripperies, but double his price? He didn't miss the frown of irritation which creased her brow briefly. He couldn't push her much longer with his silence. The outcome of this was now inevitable. He would get what he wanted, but he did need her to at least be willing if he stood any chance of getting the information he needed.

'Double what you paid and I will have a con-tract drawn up to represent your company for twelve months.'

'You are desperate, aren't you? Maybe it's a bit more than just a trinket.' He couldn't help but goad her, just to see those sparks of anger fly in her eyes.

'It's a whole lot more, but I wouldn't expect a man like you to understand.' The barb of her words wasn't lost on him. Did she know the truth of his past? She'd already accused him of being a thief. Had she investigated far enough and found the evidence damning his character for ever?

'A man like me? And what is that supposed to mean, Ms Di Sione?' She could wait a little while longer for his answer. Then he would put his deal on the table.

'What you've just done proves you are heart-less and ruthless.' She almost spat the words at him. 'No better than a thief.'

'I don't need you to tell me that.' He fought

hard to keep the growl of anger from his voice. His destroyed childhood had made him the man he was today and he didn't need a spoilt little rich girl reminding him of his past, dragging it all back up.

'Treble what you paid,' she said flatly. 'And that's my final offer.'

'I don't think you are in a position to be making me offers, Ms Di Sione.'

'And the offer to represent your company still stands.' Her hard voice held lingering traces of desperation. This was what he originally wanted, but the stakes had suddenly become much higher. Her desire for the bracelet had raised them far more than three times the price he'd paid. She was the key to everything he hungered for. All he needed to extract revenge for his parents' needless and untimely deaths was in place, thanks to her fancy for emeralds and diamonds. He had Bianca Di Sione precisely where he wanted her and he intended to exploit that fully.

'When you've quite finished making ridiculous offers, I have a proposition to put to you.'

So this was it. The moment he finally made his intentions clear, and she was sure she wasn't going to like the terms of his so-called proposition. Bianca could hardly believe this was happening. If it hadn't been for the family selling the bracelet, insisting on it going to auction, she would never have ended up in this position. Beholden to a man who unnerved her yet excited her at the same time.

She looked at Liev, an uncomfortable suspicion settling over her once more. Why was he here—buying jewellery? He must have known she wanted the bracelet, known that she would be at the auction. How had he found out and, more importantly, what was in it for him?

She inhaled, trying to instil calm into her jangled nerves. Allowing him to see just how annoyed she was would only give him more power over her—and he had enough of that already. 'And what is this deal, Mr Dragunov?'

'I need acceptance.' The cold words smarted with fury as she sensed the tension in his body. Despite the world revolving so closely around them, the throng of people attending the auction, it seemed as if they were alone, as if somehow she had connected to him on a level she'd never before experienced.

Such a thought only served to heighten her awareness of him. Or was that her shock and anger at what had just happened? The bracelet she'd promised her grandfather she'd get for him had slipped through her fingers. Straight into the hands of a ruthless Russian billionaire with a hidden agenda.

'Acceptance from who?' The unguarded question came out as she tried to make sense of all he was saying. He must have set this up. But why? Hers wasn't the only PR company in New York capable of promoting his company. Why was he obsessed with securing a contract with her?

'Society.' The word was fired harshly at her, his accent more noticeable. As was his anger.

'You can't buy that.' She thought of her life growing up in that very society, accepted simply because she'd been born into its ranks. But she'd also seen those ranks close against outsiders. It wouldn't matter how much money a man or woman had; it would take much more than that to infiltrate the elite of New York.

'Precisely. Which is why I need you.' He fixed her with a cold glare which sent a shiver of apprehension rushing down her spine. Whatever his reasons for wanting acceptance in society, he was hell-bent on achieving it.

'Me?' Still stunned from the deal he'd put to her, she couldn't form a sentence. She was good at her job. Damn good, but what he asked was a tall order, professionally as well as personally.

She didn't have the power to gain him the acceptance he craved. It was her grandfather who held all the power in her family. Or Alessandro as the eldest grandson. She was just one of three Di Sione daughters whose parents had been killed tragically when she was only two. She wasn't even the eldest daughter. How could she possibly gain this man acceptance among those she'd grown up with?

'I need you at my side. You will be my key to their world.'

His icy grey eyes held hers, and if it hadn't been for the harsh seriousness in them she would have laughed. 'Seriously, you have picked on the wrong person if you think I have enough influence to give you standing within New York society.'

The hint of laughter in her voice served only to irritate him further. She could sense it with every nerve in her body and shivered.

'You can if you are my fiancée, and the announcement of our engagement will be the first step towards that change.'

'Our engagement!' She almost choked over the words. 'We are not, under any circumstances, going to become engaged.'

He moved closer to her, intent clearly etched on his face. She wanted to back away, to remove herself from danger, but if there was one thing her past had taught her, it was to face things sooner rather than later. As this thought raced through her mind, he laid out the final terms of his deal.

'If you want to stand any chance of getting your precious bracelet back, we *will* become engaged.' He said the words so softly, all but whispering them in her ear, that to anyone watching they would have looked like lovers. She backed away, bumping into someone passing behind her. She didn't apologise. She couldn't speak. All she could think of was his cruel terms.

'What?' Finally she managed to speak, the word so loud people nearby glanced over at them. She tried to decipher what he'd said, but her mind was so shocked and muddled it was impossible.

'We will become engaged.'

'I have no intention of becoming engaged and certainly not to a man like you.' She glared angrily at him, totally shocked he could even be suggesting such a thing just to gain entry into a world he was obviously not born into. A world he didn't belong to.

'A man like me? A thief and a nobody?' He snarled the words at her, his voice a low growl, laced with menace.

She lifted her chin, not wanting to show him her fear. 'That's not what I meant and you know it.'

'For your information, if I had a choice, I would not be engaged to a spoilt little rich girl such as yourself.'

She smarted at his inference that she was materialistic and counted every last gem and diamond she owned. It was so far from the truth it was laughable, but right now she couldn't laugh.

'Then why an engagement?'

'It is a means to an end. After three months of our engagement, during which you will ensure the doors of New York society open to me, you will have your bracelet.'

'No.' She was aghast. She'd already worked out he wanted to use the bracelet as leverage to his own ends, but an engagement? 'We can never be engaged. There must be another way.'

'You said yourself that you alone at my side wouldn't achieve my aims.' His voice was calm and steady. The idea of fooling all of New York's society obviously didn't bother him as it did her. How could she go out and face them as his fiancée?

He'd lured her into the biggest trap she'd ever seen and she'd inadvertently set it herself, giving him all the ammunition he needed. Her first instinct about him had been right. He was trouble. Ruthless trouble.

'I won't do it.'

'Then you will not be able to add the bracelet to your collection of trinkets.' He raised his brows and a cruel smile spread over his lips.

'You purposefully bid for something I wanted just to satisfy your own greed?'

'Yes.' He wasn't at all shamed by her statement—if anything, he was proud of it.

'That's blackmail.' She raged against him and the injustice of it all. What was she going to tell her grandfather now?

'Not blackmail, Ms Di Sione. Business. Now do we have a deal?'

Liev watched the horrified realisation spread across Bianca's face. Waiting for her answer was merely a formality. There was no question as to what it would be. Whatever that bracelet represented, the one that had already cost him far more than he'd bid for it, her answer was going to be the same.

'If I say no, that I won't become your fake fiancée, that I will find someone else to play that part, will you allow me to buy the bracelet? Today?'

He couldn't believe she'd asked that, but he liked the phrase *fake fiancée*. That part of his plan for revenge had only emerged after he'd overheard her talking to her sister in the private lounge in Geneva. Each time she'd placed a bid she'd backed up that snippet of conversation. She would do anything to get that bracelet and obviously wasn't familiar with poker because all her emotions had been visible on her face as she'd bid.

'Absolutely not.' He spoke calmly, assured that with Bianca as his fiancée instead of merely his current date, his acceptance in society would be quicker, and what better way was there of gaining the information he needed on her brother's company and getting to the person responsible for his father's downfall?

'I suspected you were ruthless, but this is barbaric.' She spat the words at him, reminding him of the feral cats he'd shared the streets with when he'd been little more than a boy.

'Correct me if I'm wrong, Ms Di Sione, but you do not have a significant other in your life, nor have you had for many years.' He watched her eyes narrow in suspicion, and a flicker of a smile pulled at the corners of his mouth. Briefly he considered what it would be like to be the man in her life. She was so icy cold, so inaccessible, he was sure that when the sparks of passion flew they would be earth-shattering. But he'd fallen prey to one such woman before and had no intention of doing so again.

'That has nothing to do with this.'

'Ah, but it does. How can we convincingly become engaged if it is believed you are in love with another man?'

He felt a small tug at his conscience as she fought to control the panic that was clear on her pale face. The idea of being engaged to him obviously horrified her and he wondered just who would be her chosen man.

'There must be someone else. I can't be the only person who can propel you into society.' Bianca looked at him, hardly able to believe he was serious. His stance and his hardened expression left her in no doubt how serious he was. He meant every word. It was the only way of getting the bracelet, and hadn't she admitted to herself she'd do anything to get it?

'No. Not if you want the bracelet.'

'You are the lowest.' She wanted to hiss at

him, to let him know just how angry she was, but astutely she realised that would give the bracelet even more importance in his eyes. He must never know exactly how much she wanted it—or why. If he knew that, he would have all the power.

'It has been said.' His cold, somewhat distant reply didn't make sense, but she didn't care about what he felt. All she cared about was fulfilling Grandfather's last wishes. If she had to do it this way, then so be it—for now at least. She would do everything she could, as quickly as she could, to give this man what he wanted. But did she trust him to keep his word?

'It will never, under any circumstances, be a proper engagement. It will certainly not last any longer than three months, after which time you will give me the bracelet.' She set out her terms. Events of ten years ago and the bets that had been placed on her at the prom, by the man she'd loved from afar, surfaced like demons from the past.

She thought she was over that humiliation. It had scarred her emotionally, making her determined to keep men locked out of her heart. She'd walked away from that experience a virgin, her reputation intact and with a vow never to be so naive again, and had been unable to trust a man since. And she certainly didn't trust Liev Dragunov one bit. Not when he had the one thing she had to have, giving her little choice but to agree to his terms.

'In fact,' she began again before he could say anything, 'if you achieve your objectives before that time, our *engagement* will end and you will give me the bracelet.'

'You sound sure you can do this.' His voice held a note of suspicion as she looked up at him, resisting the urge to just walk away and forget it all. But she couldn't. She had to do this—and she would.

'The only problem I have will be convincing everyone I have fallen for such a...' She floundered over her words, hating herself for it.

'Such a what?'

She looked at him. Everything about him shouted wealth and power, but it couldn't hide the untamed man within. It was something that would attract women, but she was not one of those women. Never had been and never would be.

'A ruthless rebel.' He actually laughed, as if he was proud of it.

'Do I have your word? Three months at the most.'

'You have my word—you will have the

bracelet before three months, providing sufficient acceptance of my name and standing in society have been achieved.'

'And if that doesn't happen?' She knew the answer already.

'You will not see the bracelet again, but I am sure with your excellent PR skills you can smooth the way for me.'

She hated him more than she'd hated any man before. But unlike the last time she'd been set up ten years ago, there wasn't a way out. At least, not an obvious one. She was dealing with a much more determined character this time. A force of nature let loose on her Achilles heel. Her grandfather.

'Three months. Not a day more,' she reiterated firmly.

'Yes.' His Russian accent, which had softened as he'd whispered his terms in her ear, was suddenly very distinctive again.

'And when do you propose this fake engagement to start?' That choice of word wasn't lost on her as she wondered how her brothers and sisters would take the news of her engagement. Especially Allegra, who knew all the sordid details of the prom and why she'd sworn never to get involved with men. How could she tell her it was all for show, that in order to get the bracelet Grandfather so desperately wanted, she was bargaining with her reputation?

She thought again of how tired and worn out Allegra had looked in Geneva and knew that, whatever happened, she couldn't confide in her. Not now. This was something she would have to face alone.

She looked directly into Liev's cold grey eyes, determined not to let her unease show.

'It will start right now.'

CHAPTER THREE

LIEV WAS CONVINCED the fiery woman who had just challenged him so passionately hadn't really agreed to his terms. Not completely. Her dark eyes met and held his defiantly, and he knew she was still trying to figure an alternative way out. Playing for time.

All he needed was to discover why the bracelet was so important, why she would even agree to such a drastic deal for a piece of jewellery. But that wasn't so urgent now. He needed to set the stage for their engagement and it would have to be convincing.

'Right now we could certainly pass for lovers who have had a tiff, but you are going to have to do better if we are to convince everyone that we are madly in love and have just got engaged.'

'Madly in love?' The surprise in her voice echoed that in her expression.

'Yes, Bianca, madly in love. That way my acceptance into society is more guaranteed. Do you think you can portray a woman in love?' He lowered his voice and taunted her mercilessly, enjoying all but whispering in her ear. Her scent filled him, knocking his heightened senses off balance.

'Don't worry about that, Mr Dragunov. I've spent my life in the limelight. I can act my part.' Bianca's words, once again, cut short his runaway thoughts.

He nodded his approval. 'In that case, you will have no objection to me putting my arm around your shoulders as we leave and, naturally, as we are in love, you will welcome it. You will look happy. Ecstatic. I have, after all, just bought you an expensive gift—and, most importantly, you will call me Liev.'

'Where are we going?' For a moment she looked startled and again his conscience snagged on something, but he quickly reminded himself this icy beauty was agreeing to his proposition for a frivolous trinket. Diamonds and emeralds it may be, but it was frivolous nonetheless. She was exactly the kind of woman he despised and there was only one reason for being here with her—the revenge he had to exact on the company her brother now headed. The one that was responsible for his family's ruin.

He smiled and moved closer in the way a lover would do, pushing back the hurt from the past in order to play his part. He caught the scent of her perfume again and this time inhaled, closing his eyes momentarily, enjoying the scent of summer roses. There were going to be parts to this revenge he would enjoy immensely.

'First of all, as we leave we will have to pass the press that will most probably have gathered to find out who it was that made such an outrageously high bid on the bracelet. Then we will find a quiet bar to finalise the finer points of our deal.'

'Don't worry, Mr Dragunov. I can handle the press.' Her flippant tone made him smile, admiring the fight that still raged in her.

'I have every reason to believe you can.' The slight widening of her eyes, which turned into a deep blue, reminding him of the dark waters of the ocean, suggested she hadn't thought about the possibility that the press would be outside, despite her bravado. But he had. And he intended this to be the first time they were noticed together as a couple. 'It will set things up nicely for an engagement announcement.'

'You're actually serious about the engagement?' Incredulity filled her voice.

'I am nothing if not serious, Bianca.'

The use of her name sent a rush of awareness through him, probably because of the way she drew in a sharp breath, her luscious lips looking ever more kissable. The inconvenient pull of attraction to the woman who was the key to successfully avenging his parents was not something he'd considered. Nor would he do so again. Complete focus was all he needed to maintain. Any other emotion was surplus to requirements—just as it had always been.

'There is a bar on the next block that will be quiet enough for us to discuss the finer details of our arrangement.' He took her hand and felt her hesitation as she allowed him to wrap his fingers tightly around it.

'What about the bracelet?' So she didn't trust him.

'It is quite safe and will remain that way until our arrangement is complete.' Without further comment, he walked towards the main doors of the auction house. As the door was opened for them, he let her hand go and put his arm around her shoulders, pulling her snugly against his body.

It felt good to have her there, where he could

feel every step she took and every curve of her body. The flash of the cameras lit up the early evening and satisfaction raced through him. What would make the headlines? The highest bid so far this year at the auction house or Bianca Di Sione out with a Russian billionaire? Either way it suited him. He walked Bianca through the throng and hailed a taxi.

Bianca quickly got into the back of the car, glad to be out of the glare of the flashlights. Being the focus of press attention wasn't new for her. She'd been all but hounded by them for as long as she could remember. Such attention certainly hadn't been courted, but was more something she'd learnt to deal with—and avoid where possible.

She looked at Liev as he got in beside her, still unable to believe what had happened. He calmly gave an address and sat back next to her, seemingly happy that they had been photographed together. Having him so close was distracting and she had to resist the need to slide along the seat, further away from him. Her heart also thumped a little harder, making her feel light-headed. What was the matter with her?

'So you've been photographed as my companion. What's next, Mr Dragunov? Have you already chosen a fake engagement ring?' She couldn't keep the flippant tone from her voice. Was it born out of panic to her reaction to being near him or was it the situation she now found herself in? Her anger rose once more, fired up by her confusion, and together they made a heady cocktail. How could she find a man attractive and hate him at the same time?

'As a matter of fact, I have.' He startled her from her thoughts and she looked at him, the golden sunshine of New York's summer evening playing across the sculpted contours of his face, lending him a dangerous edge. He dominated the very air she breathed as she sat next to him, trying to ignore the tingle of awareness from just being close to him. 'But it is far from fake.'

Frustration fired through her, making her snap. 'I can't believe you are doing all this just because I declined to represent your company.'

'That was a minor inconvenience and not at all my main goal.' He looked at her, his eyes hard as they met hers. Everything else slipped into non-existence for the second time that day and mentally she shook herself. Where was the unflappable Bianca who'd forged her way through life for the past ten years without love and definitely without this kind of physical attraction?

'What is your main goal, Mr Dragunov?' She forced her mind to focus. This was one man she had to be on full alert with. He'd already proved that.

'Liev.'

Good grief, even hearing him say his name was sexy. She had to stop thinking such things right now. She had to get a grip and pull herself together. She already knew the consequences of letting emotions show and wasn't this proposition a battle? One she had every intention of fighting.

She recalled what she'd told Allegra—that she'd do anything to get the bracelet for her grandfather. It seemed that Liev was going to test that claim to the full, but she wouldn't be thwarted by such an arrogant man. She would do whatever necessary to get that bracelet from him—even a fake engagement.

Her usual cool composure was well and truly ruffled. It was like going back to that prom night when she'd almost allowed herself to be used in the most basic way. She had been a challenge just because of her family name, one she'd risen to and overcome in spectacular style, maintaining her reputation and destroying that of the boy she'd foolishly believed she'd loved.

Since then she'd given men a wide berth, determined not to repeat the same mistake by letting anyone close, but now, confronted with a man like Liev, she had let her emotions show and everything had unravelled. But how could she not bring emotions into the task of getting back something her grandfather wanted so much after he'd told her it was his final wish?

'You must call me Liev.' The insistence in his voice was clear and she stifled a smile, knowing she was irritating him.

The taxi stopped and Liev got out. For a moment she thought about shutting the door and instructing the driver to take her home. If it had been anything else this man had taken from her, she would have done just that, but the bracelet was her grandfather's dying wish. She couldn't let Liev walk away with the one thing which would make her grandfather happy in his last days. She just wished she knew why it was so important to the elderly man.

Neither Matteo nor Allegra had heard the full story when he'd set them similar tasks. All they knew was that each item was a Lost Mistress from the tales he'd told them as children, as if they were part of the Di Sione fairy tale.

Bianca got out of the taxi onto the sidewalk, the hum of the traffic and the sound of sirens overpowering her. Or was it the man who stood watching her? His eagle-like assessment was unnerving.

'You made a wise choice.' His voice was deep and firm and she frowned at him, but before she could ask what he meant, he continued. 'Not leaving in that taxi.'

'I was tempted, and believe me, if there was another way, I would have done exactly that,' she snapped back. 'But we have to settle the details of our deal first and I warn you, *Liev*. I *will* go if those finer details aren't mutually beneficial.'

She wanted to tell him that the bracelet didn't mean that much to her, that he'd got it all wrong about her being the spoilt little rich girl, but suspected it would only draw his attention to it once more. If he could put a deal like that on the table, he could do anything. She had to keep her guard up.

'And believe me, Bianca, they will be.' The way he said her name, caressing it even while his voice remained granite hard, sent a shiver over her as if he'd actually touched her—and she hated him for it.

She walked into the bar with Liev, not completely unaware of the glances cast in their direction or the way he attracted the attention of just about every female in the bar. He was handsome, that was undisputable, but in a hard and angry kind of way. Or did he just hate her because he thought she was privileged and spoilt? He'd made no secret of his opinion of her.

She drew in a sharp breath as he placed his hand in the small of her back, guiding her to a table set back from the rest of the bar, the privacy it would afford them undoubted. Had he planned this evening down to such a level? Her earlier suspicions surfaced and she became more convinced that he'd known she would be at the auction. She bit down on the anger which bubbled up from deep within.

She slid along the seat, hoping he would sit opposite her, not quite able to take being close to him again so soon after the short journey in the taxi. She still couldn't understand the effect he had on her, how heat could infuse her so quickly just from being close to him. She'd resisted the pull of sexual chemistry for the past ten years and she could continue to do so now. If Liev thought charm would soften his twisted deal, he was very much mistaken. She was immune to such tactics.

'This is very, how shall I say, convenient.' Her words were spiked with tartness as she desperately fought to suppress that new idea of awareness to a man she'd disliked on first sight and now hated with a vengeance.

He flicked his brows up at her sarcasm, then signalled to the bar staff. A bottle of wine, her favourite red, arrived promptly. That uncomfortable suspicion returned. He seemed to know a lot about her. Far too much.

'I pride myself on being able to prepare for every eventuality.' The self-satisfied expression on his face just begged to be wiped away, and she vowed that before this deal was over she would do just that.

'In that case, why not allow me to find a more suitable fiancée for you, one more powerful, more able to open the doors you so desperately want opened? You overestimate my standing in the Di Sione family if you think an engagement to me will do all you want.'

'Not only is it your family's name and that old-money respectability I need. It's your undoubted skill in your professional life. So you see, Bianca, I have made my choice well.'

'There must be someone better placed than me for this ridiculous sham of an engagement?'

She watched as he poured two glasses of

wine, desperately trying to think of who that woman could be, knowing deep down it couldn't be her. History was repeating itself, but on a much more dramatic scale. Her family name and reputation was being used once more, callously gambled with, but this time she couldn't see any way out. Not if she wanted the bracelet.

'And who exactly would you suggest?' He leant back in his seat, his wine untouched in front of him. She had the uneasy sensation of being more like a hunting eagle's quarry, set up and unwittingly waiting for the moment she would be swept away from all she'd ever known and devoured.

'I will find someone.' She could hear the desperation in her voice. Could he hear it too? 'There are agencies, although how they'd look upon the request for a fake fiancée, I don't know.'

She tried hard to think who it could be, but single women able to offer him what he wanted were few, and those she could think of wouldn't stand a chance against his lethal charm. She had no need to be close to a man, so maybe she was the best woman for the job.

He folded one arm across his body and raised one to his face, his thumb on his chin and his finger rasping over the hints of stubble; the sound, although hardly audible, set her nerves even more on edge. 'That won't be necessary. I am certain we can come to a mutually satisfying arrangement. I have something you want and you are in a position to give me what I want.'

'How long have you been in New York, Mr Dragunov?' She used his surname and couldn't help the smile which caught her lips at his annoyed expression. She noticed his eyes glitter, making them ice cold.

'I have been doing business here for a few years on a small scale, but now our engagement will ensure the success of my latest and biggest venture. It will turn my company global. I will still keep my main office and home in St Petersburg, where I grew up.' The last few words had a harsh edge to them that was hard to miss.

'And your family? Where do they live?'

'I have no family.'

'So there is no danger of your family finding out about this engagement?' She flung the question at him, giving voice to the concerns she had over how her family would take the news. He didn't appear at all worried about deceiving everyone.

'Not at all. My parents died when I was young.' She saw his jaw clench, saw the flash of pain in his eyes. Pain she knew only too well. Her heart twisted. He'd lost his parents too. He knew the pain she'd grown up with wishing she had known her mother and father, wishing she had more than snippets of memories.

'I'm sorry,' she said softly, not wanting to open up to him about such things. She never told anyone that she could barely recall her mother and had no memories of her father whatsoever, but hearing Liev's pain, seeing it in his eyes, opened up that shame and exposed her pain. She fought hard against the urge to confide in him, reminding herself they were not in a real relationship. This man was not to be trusted. In any way.

That connection they shared from the past still didn't alter the fact that her brothers and sisters would find out about the engagement and she wondered how she could make them believe it was real. She would be lying to them, but she had no choice. If for one moment her brothers thought she was being blackmailed, or set up, as she preferred to think of it, she was certain Liev Dragunov wouldn't be getting the acceptance in society he craved. And that would mean she wouldn't get the bracelet. She would fail her grandfather in his last wish.

That thought made sadness sweep over her and she took a sip of the wine, trying to ignore the intensity of Liev's eyes on her. She wished she could talk to Allegra. All her life she'd looked up to her as more of a mother figure than a sister, but when it came to troubles of the heart, she was always her big sister, someone she could confide in. But for the first time, that wasn't available. She was miles away in Dar-Aman with what appeared to be the love of her life.

'Losing my parents is not something I dwell on.' Liev's words, more sharply accented than usual, dragged her from her melancholy thoughts.

'You may not have family to consider, but whatever plans you have to instigate this engagement will need to be good if I am to convince my brothers and sisters that we are engaged.' She thought of their probable reaction to her even dating, let alone getting engaged. They knew she'd never taken a man home, let alone frequented the dating scene of New York.

'It will be.' His high and mighty attitude was beginning to wear thin. He was far too self-assured, far too confident she'd fall into line with his ludicrous plan.

'I'm serious, Mr Dragunov. If you want doors opened, then you first have to get past the whole Di Sione family, convince them we are in love, because they will not just accept my sudden engagement without question, not when I haven't dated in years.'

'Not dated in years? You make it sound as if you have never been in love, never had an affair.' He regarded her with suspicion and disbelief which only spiked at her irritation.

'I haven't. Not that it is any of your business, Mr Dragunov.'

'If you don't start referring to me as Liev all will be lost. No doors will be opened, which means no bracelet. I will return to St Petersburg with the bracelet and it will never again leave Russia.'

Take the bracelet back to Russia! That was something she hadn't considered at all. There was no way that bracelet was going anywhere else except to the Di Sione family estate.

Liev could see the moment Bianca finally realised he was serious. He saw her eyes wash with resignation, watched those very kissable lips press together, and it was all he could do to keep his thoughts on his mission, instead of thinking how they would feel crushed beneath his as passion burst to life between them. Did she really expect him to believe she'd never dated? A woman as beautiful as her would have exploited that beauty along with her family name and wealth, of that there was no doubt.

'I do not know why this item is so precious to you, but I mean what I say. Only when you have achieved your side of the deal will I allow you to have it. Not a moment sooner. Three months should be sufficient. Don't you think?'

He watched as the colour drained from her face, now satisfied there wouldn't be any last-minute attempts to thwart his plans. He'd waited too long for this moment, and when he'd told her of his parents he'd had to clench his hands into fists, to prevent himself from revealing the truth, from telling her that she and her brother were a crucial part of avenging their untimely deaths.

'You're despicable,' she whispered at him, her breath coming hard and fast. Better that she hated him. Hatred drove a person more than any other emotion. He'd learnt that the hard way as he'd fought and brawled—and worse—for every morsel he'd eaten since the day, at twelve years of age, he'd seen his father's coffin lowered into the ground, joining that of his mother.

'Then we have a healthy respect of one another, Bianca.' He saw her jaw clench as he used her name.

'How exactly are you going to convince the world that our engagement is real? When we obviously dislike each other so intensely?' The tartness of her words touched a raw nerve, one that had been exposed by remembering his past.

'I will give you a ring. The rest is up to you.' He thought of the large diamond ring he'd bought. Proof, if she needed it, that this whole scenario had been planned down to the last detail. But that was of no importance now; she'd agreed to the deal. He had her right where he wanted her.

As soon as he'd discovered her desperation to get the bracelet he'd done everything in his power to prevent her buying it privately, making a deal with the seller and then bidding for it all over again. It had cost him a fortune, but one he could easily stand, and he'd forced Bianca out into the open where he could snatch it away from her. It was his bargaining tool, but what he hadn't been prepared for was just how badly she wanted it.

'Up to me?' Shocked, her blue eyes widened, sending his thoughts briefly off course again.

'Yes. The sooner our engagement is known, the sooner you can gain my acceptance with the use of your family name.'

'And that's all it's about?' Her dark eyes narrowed slightly in suspicion and he wondered if he'd been too unguarded, let too much slip. It was a fine line he was walking between gaining all the information he could from her and telling her too much.

'I am to attend a charity function this Friday and you will also attend—as my fiancée.'

'So soon?'

'I intend we are seen in public as a newly engaged couple as soon as possible.'

She inhaled deeply. 'Very well. I agree but only for three months and not a day longer.'

'You will also use your business connections to introduce me to those people who would be most influential in establishing my company here in New York.' He pressed home the need to be accepted by society, which whilst being beneficial, it was not the main purpose for his deal. The main purpose was to extract information from Bianca about Dario Di Sione and the finer details of ICE, the company he intended to bring down.

She sighed as if bored with the whole discussion—or was it resigned to her fate? 'I will also expect you to ensure our engagement is as public as possible and gains the interest of not only society, but the press, although I do have a few plans for that myself.'

'So you want me to act the adoring fiancée in public, pose for the press at every opportunity and arrange a PR campaign that will launch you and your business into the heart of New York's business world?'

'That is exactly what I want, Bianca.'

CHAPTER FOUR

BIANCA HADN'T HEARD from Liev since the day of the auction, but the idea that he had forgotten about their first public date this evening wasn't a comfort she could afford. For the best part of the past week she'd looked at every other way possible to get out of the deal she'd been forced to accept, but nothing had presented itself. If she wanted the bracelet she didn't have a choice.

Already photos of them leaving the auction and Liev's high bid for the bracelet had caused a stir, alerting the gossip columns to a blooming romance. They'd speculated if the self-made Russian billionaire was the man to melt the sleeping heart of Bianca Di Sione, labouring hard on the fact that she'd not been seen out with male company for many years.

With no other way of getting the bracelet, Bianca knew she and Liev needed to be seen together again, and when they were, it would make the next piece of their engagement story. She stood at her apartment window, looking out over the city of New York as it basked in the sunshine of a July evening, willing Liev to arrive. She just wanted to get this evening over with.

He had chosen one of society's biggest and most well-attended charity parties at which to parade her as his fiancée. Inside she was all nerves, wanting to do nothing other than run and hide, but outside, as ever, she was cool, calm and sophisticated. She'd hidden her vulnerabilities further with heavy eye make-up and dark lipstick—very much her preferred mask to hide behind.

The firm knock on her apartment door made her jump like a nervous kitten. That had to stop. There was no way she was going to allow Liev to see how anxious she really was. This was all just business, and the fact that it reminded her so starkly of her prom night had to be pushed aside; otherwise she'd never be able to put on the required act of adoration.

She picked up her clutch bag and headed for the front door, the silk of her dress sighing softly as she moved. At the door she took another deep breath, then looked out through the spyhole. Liev's broad shoulders and hardened yet handsome face filled it. She drew in a sharp and ragged breath.

The way she reacted to him only made this more difficult. There had only been one other man who'd caused that kind of kick to her heart rate and he'd done nothing but humiliate her, betting with his friends he'd take her virginity the night of her prom. He hadn't, but that night had only made her more determined to give it to the right man—and she hadn't met him yet.

'You can do this, Bianca. You have to,' she whispered sternly, pushing back the past. She lifted her chin, put her shoulders back and pinned on a smile before opening the door.

Liev stood there in all his male glory, dressed in a tuxedo and looking so damn good she couldn't drag her gaze from him. He in turn allowed his unconcealed scrutiny to travel down the length of the emerald green silk dress which clung seductively to her, before slowly moving back to her face.

She met his gaze with a haughty expression. 'I trust this meets with your approval.'

He nodded and his cold grey eyes looked directly into hers as his superiority radiated off him in waves, irritating her further. 'Yes. Exactly right.'

Bianca marvelled at the fact that he hadn't actually dictated how she should dress, but then maybe even he had thought that was a step too far. She knew they would create a stunning couple and was certain they would end up in one of the celebrity magazines. But being seen and photographed with him was the easy part.

Tonight, if their sudden engagement wasn't to be questioned by her family, she would have to act like a woman in love, swept away by Liev's commanding presence. If one hint of their deal showed, Liev would find the doors he wanted opened slamming in his face and she would lose the one thing she just had to have.

'But there is something missing.'

'There is?' She stumbled over her words again. What had she forgotten? She'd made sure every part of her act was right.

He stepped towards her, getting too close. From his inside jacket pocket he pulled out what could only be a ring box. Her heart turned over. The fake engagement ring.

'You cannot truly be my fiancée without this.'

Cautiously she took the box from him. This had never been how she'd imagined the moment a man would propose. Their fingers brushed and her gaze shot up to meet his. The air around them sparked, as if a bolt of lightning had struck. He held her gaze as she glared angrily back at him.

She opened the box, trying to ignore the pounding of her heart, and gasped as a large diamond glittered expensively. 'Where did you get this?'

'Another auction. Like you, I have a liking for the finer things in life.'

She looked at the diamond glinting at her. 'I can't wear this.'

'You can and you will.' He took it from the box and lifted her hand, sliding the ring onto her finger in silence. She couldn't help but watch and wish things were different.

The single large diamond which sparkled in the light as she moved was hardly going to go unnoticed this evening. By tomorrow morning, news of their engagement would be sweeping across the city and she still hadn't found the courage to tell any of her family.

'We should go.' She had to move on from this moment and the crushed dreams it represented. Remember why she was doing it.

She stepped past him, unable to meet his gaze, and pulled her door shut, desperate to avoid any further contact when so much of her skin was exposed, and briefly wished she'd selected a more modest dress. But with a role to play, this had been the best choice.

That wish intensified when seconds later they were enclosed in the elevator as it descended. The shiny interior reflected their images as they stood side by side. She tried not to look and to calm her breathing, but the harshness of his reflected expression did little to help. If he was going to scowl like that, how would anyone really believe they were engaged? As their eyes met in the reflection, she realised she had to do more than dress the part of a woman in love—she had to act it too.

'My car is waiting. When we arrive I hope that you will appear more enamoured with me, instead of visibly flinching from my touch.' His words mirrored her worries and were sharp, his accent more pronounced. She had to stifle a smile at the knowledge that she was irritating him and resist the urge to continue to do so. Rebellion wouldn't help her at all.

'If I can take that constant frown from your face, then there will be no doubt in anyone's mind that we are in love.' Her tart words hit their target and he turned to look at her, his eyes narrowing in suspicion.

'Already we make a well-matched couple. Let's ensure that others see something softer, something more akin to a fairy-tale romance.' His acerbic tone almost stole her breath as she glared back at him, frustration bubbling inside her.

So he wanted fairy tale, did he? 'Very well, then that is what you shall have.'

The elevator doors opened and she looked up at him, slid her arm into his and pulled her body against him. The heat that seared her skin made her draw in a sharp breath—as did the racing of her pulse. What was the matter with her? Since when did any man do that to her? Certainly not since the night of her high school prom.

'I am pleased we are… How do you say…? On the same page.' His commanding voice had suddenly taken on a deep sexy tone as he seemed to scrabble for the right English expression. But it was a tone she would do well to ignore if the skittering of her heart was anything to go by.

'We both have something the other wants. That is as far as our connection goes.' She glanced up at his profile to see the corner of his mouth twitch with the beginnings of a smile.

With her head held high and her arm in

Liev's, she walked through the lobby, giving the doorman a smile, and out into the warmth of the evening. Before she had time to think, a chauffeur had opened the back door of a limousine and Liev was helping her in. She slid across the seat with as much composure as her tight-fitting dress would allow, only to be joined seconds later by Liev. The close proximity of the car was far more daunting than the elevator.

'When we arrive, it is my hope that we will be photographed together and that this...' He lifted her left hand, the large diamond sparkling mischievously. 'I hope this will not go unnoticed.'

'I don't think there is any question it will not be noticed.' Her pulse leapt again as he held her hand by her fingertips, his sharp gaze holding hers captive. Boldly she looked into the cold grey of his eyes, noticing again those flecks of blue.

'I am counting on it, Bianca. I need to enter your social circle as much as you need that bracelet.' The drawl of his voice sent a chill down her spine as cold as the heat which sizzled up her arm from just the touch of his hand on hers.

Before she could say anything else, the limousine pulled up at the doors of one of New York's most prestigious hotels. Through the darkened windows she could see crowds had assembled along with hordes of paparazzi. Liev would get his wish.

More exposed and vulnerable than she'd ever felt, she stepped out of the car, followed by Liev. The flashlights burst into action as he put his arm around her waist, drawing her so close to him. Much closer than she'd dared to be moments before in the elevator.

Liev held Bianca close, enjoying the sensation of her body against his once more. When she'd moved against him as they had left the elevator, he'd been shocked. It was the last thing he expected of the cool and level-headed business-woman. To find she had a playful, even flirta-tious streak was unexpected and not totally unwelcome. Maybe his new engagement would prove more entertaining than he'd planned.

'Bianca. Whose ring is that?' Once one of the paparazzi had spotted the ring, the cam-eras exploded.

'Thank you,' he said firmly, stepping in front of her, gallantly shielding her from more opportune shots. 'All will be revealed in good time.'

With that he guided her towards the door of the hotel and into the relative calm beyond its doors. His plan was well and truly under way. He looked across at Bianca as she stopped and was shocked to see vulnerability on her face, but as she sensed him watching her, that slipped away to be replaced by the toughness he would have expected from the woman he'd come to know and even admire.

'Well, that is one hurdle over.' She feigned an interest in smoothing the silk of her dress down against her body. He gritted his teeth together as he watched her, unable to drag his gaze away from her. Did she have any idea how flirtatious that action was? 'Our engagement will no longer be a secret. It would, however, have been nice to have had time to prepare my family.'

'Why? Would you have had time to think of them if we had been swept away by the madness of love?'

'I don't think the madness of love sweeping me away is something any of them will believe, especially my brother Dario, whose launch I am at this moment supposed to be concentrating on.' Her eyes sparked with angry fury as she turned to look at him, her voice low and hushed as she spoke, but he didn't miss the resentment in it.

'I'm sure they will forgive you.' He wanted to ask about her brother. She'd given him the perfect opportunity to find out more of Dario Di Sione's dealings, but as ever, he would have to bide his time and wait. Now was not the time and place, and neither was her mood conducive to sharing such information. It was far better she was lulled into a false sense of security.

As they entered the room, she became the Bianca he'd first met, the confident woman who knew what she wanted and how to get it. It reminded him that right now she wanted the bracelet and the only way to get it was to introduce him into her world and that if she had a choice she would not be spending the evening with him.

'Bianca.' He watched as a woman, several years younger than Bianca, kissed her on each cheek and smiled at her. 'How are those twin brothers of yours? Doing well by all accounts.'

Liev's interest was piqued. One of those twin brothers was the reason he was here. Dario was now the owner of ICE, one of the most well-known computer companies which had become rich and successful by buying out other companies, then closing out the founders, destroying them until they had nothing. Just as they had done to his father.

Whilst Liev accepted that Dario hadn't been responsible for the buyout which destroyed his father, he'd certainly turned a blind eye to the company's past. Now, through Dario, Liev intended to expose all those underhand deals and the man who'd been behind them all.

'Yes, they are. In fact, Dario is soon launching a new product.' Bianca's reply drew him back from the black hole of his childhood, her sweet voice full of pride. But how could she be proud of a man who advocated such practices? 'This is Liev Dragunov, my…'

Bianca's voice faltered very briefly, but he wasn't going to give her the opportunity to create the wrong kind of speculation. 'Her fiancé.'

'Oh, Bianca, that's so exciting.' The younger woman beamed, probably because she was now in possession of one of the best bits of gossip this evening. He knew how women's minds worked.

'Yes, isn't it?' Bianca bounced back, her smile firmly planted on those painted red lips.

'And what a ring.' The woman cooed.

Bianca unashamedly showed off the large diamond ring he'd bought for the purpose. Every dollar it had cost proving to be a worthwhile investment.

'We should take our seats, my love.' Liev

spoke softly and smiled down at her face as she turned to look up at him. Briefly her eyes filled with question, and then she smiled. A knowing smile that told him she knew exactly what he was doing.

'Yes, darling,' she said huskily, then turned back to the other woman. 'It's so nice to be looked after.'

Liev guided her through the guests, aware of the curious glances of women and the sometimes suspicious glares of the men. He knew that without Bianca he would never be accepted into their world, no matter how many millions he had. They closed ranks against strangers and self-made men like him, but with her at his side, those ranks were beginning to move apart.

Bianca seated herself at her designated table. Her name-card nestling close to Liev's seemed strangely intimate, and as it had done when she'd first opened her apartment door this evening, her pulse began to race erratically, unsettling her more than she cared to admit.

He stood behind her as she took her seat and rested his hand on the back of her chair, leaning down to bring his head close to hers. She turned to look at him, startled by the realisation that she was close enough to kiss him. What would his kiss be like? Brief and cold or hard and demanding? Either would suit him. He smiled at her and she seriously wondered if he was second-guessing her thoughts. She blushed, worried that he knew she was thinking about kissing him.

'You look beautiful this evening.' His voice was deep and sultry and a new kind of intensity filled those icy grey eyes, warming them so they resembled the ocean as the sun's midday rays danced on it.

'Thank you.' She wanted to lower her gaze, to break the tension which suddenly seemed to zip between them. She would have to be cautious. Liev Dragunov, her three-month fiancé and blackmailer, possessed charms that could be lethal to an inexperienced heart such as hers. A heart that had been torn apart by deceit and disappointment before it had even had the chance to truly experience love.

Strangely self-conscious, she looked away as more guests arrived at their table, and very soon the intimacy they'd just experienced was lost in a flow of conversation. Liev became immersed in a discussion with the other men and she was surprised to hear the pride in his voice when he spoke of his company.

She tried to concentrate on the women's talk of the latest Broadway show but she couldn't help listening to Liev, wishing he was talking to her like that. She felt the barriers she always kept well and truly up lowering as her curiosity increased about the man she was now engaged to. Sitting at the table, with others about them, she was more relaxed about being in his company, somehow tuned into his mood.

By the end of the meal she'd heard enough snippets of conversation to have built up a good picture of him, something she liked to do before representing a new client, but never before had she heard it indirectly from the client themselves. It was also what she'd tried to do when he'd initially contacted her. She recalled that gut instinct she'd had that there was more to him than he let anyone see and that he was as determined as he was unstoppable.

Now, to her cost, she knew that to be true. Liev Dragunov would stop at nothing to get what he wanted.

'It has been a very successful evening.' He took her hand from where it rested on her lap, startling her out of her thoughts. She glanced around to see just one of the four couples who'd joined them at their table remained, deep in their own conversation.

'Yes.' She forced the word out, but it sounded like a husky whisper, so she fixed him with a bold glare, only to find that smile which never fully showed tugging at the corners of his lips. 'I'd like to go home now. I have a busy day tomorrow preparing for a customer launch.'

'Your brother?' His thumb caressed her hand, making her skin tingle and distracting her far too much, but his voice had a granite-hard edge to it.

'Yes. As you obviously overheard earlier, my brother Dario is launching a new product next month.' Irritated that he'd listened to her conversation, she snapped the words out. For some absurd reason, she didn't want him to know anything about her family. It wasn't as if they were really engaged. All she was doing was opening doors for him.

'You, too, overheard much of my conversation if I'm not mistaken, Bianca.' The feral warning in his eyes made them glint like ice in the morning sun, but she refused to be intimated by him. Blackmail was enough.

'I didn't realise you'd built your business up from nothing.' Her honest curiosity got the better of her as did the need to rein in the increasing tension. 'You will, of course, need to tell me more about yourself if I am to represent your company.'

'Providing you tell me more about yourself.' His eyes flared briefly with amusement, like a firework before it melted into the night sky.

'I don't think so.' There was no way she was going to open up to this man and tell him about her family. She didn't want to reveal the nightmare of losing her parents when she was so very young and the difficulty of growing up in the spotlight without them. He probably knew already, but she didn't want to have to tell him anything. 'I'd like to go home now.'

'Very well.' He stood up and she suddenly became overwhelmed by him. As she sat there and looked at him, at the broad width of his shoulders, she felt almost helpless, as if he'd somehow taken every last bit of control from her. She didn't like it one bit. Just as Dominic had done, he was using her for who she was, what she could offer him. The only difference this time—Liev had something she needed.

She stood up, her height in heels almost coming close to matching his, but when he put his arm around her back, his hand resting on her waist and pulling her against him, she knew her ability to hold it all together much longer was slipping away. He was eroding her ever-present mask of confidence faster than the tide wiped away footprints in the sand.

'I will get a taxi.' All she wanted was to be on her own, to cease this charade of new-found love.

'What kind of fiancé would that make me if I allowed you to go home alone in a taxi? I will at least take you to your door, Bianca.'

Aware that they were being watched and that getting the bracelet back rested on how quickly he was accepted by people like these, she smiled sweetly at him, placing her hand on his arm and leaning against him seductively. 'I can't think of anything better.'

His finger tipped up her chin, forcing her to look directly into the icy heart of his eyes. The world around them stopped turning and nothing else existed. The glamour of the room and everyone in it faded away. All she could see was the handsome man who had claimed her as his fake fiancée. All she could hear was the hard thudding of her heart. All she could feel was the heat of his body.

'It will be my pleasure.' He lowered his head and before she could do anything his lips met hers. Instinctively she closed her eyes as her body swayed towards him and hated herself for it. Her heart rate accelerated wildly and heat surged from deep within her as he moved his lips against hers, teasing and coaxing a response from her. She couldn't help herself as butterflies took flight in her stomach; she sighed softly, enjoying the sensation of his kiss, of knowing that he, too, enjoyed it.

As all those conflicting sensations whirled around inside her, he pulled back just enough to whisper, 'And a very great honour.'

Those huskily whispered words pulled her back from insanity.

'I don't think you know the meaning of that word.' Her low retort had a sharpened edge to it and she wanted to collapse back onto her chair with relief when he let her go.

Before he could say or do anything else, she walked out of the room, away from the watchful eyes of people she'd known all her life and away from whatever it was that had just happened between her and the man she supposedly hated.

Liev got out of the limousine and helped Bianca out. The night air was warm and, as ever, the city hummed with activity. Bianca was still all fiery control and simmering sexiness, testing him more than he'd ever thought possible. Just as that kiss had done. He could still feel her lips against his, still hear that soft sigh of contentment. For a brief moment he had melted her icy heart.

'There is no need to come up with me.' Her words were so cold they almost froze him out, and he wondered about the passionate woman he'd glimpsed as his lips had brushed hers. Did she ever let her guard down enough for that passion to take over? Was that why she hadn't dated recently? The challenge to find out more about the ice princess was immense, but it would get in the way of his real purpose and he couldn't be distracted by a beautiful woman, no matter how attractive the prospect was.

'We need to arrange our next date,' he said as he held open the lobby door for her and nodded at the doorman.

As they waited for the elevator, he thought of seeing Bianca again. He pushed aside thoughts of kisses and passion, focusing instead on the thrill of sparring with her. The thought of coming closer to the moment he could avenge his father's demise by finding out about Dario Di Sione's latest product launch and using it against ICE pushed him forward even though his conscience was beginning to tug with something he didn't want to acknowledge.

The elevator doors swished open and he followed Bianca in, more aware than ever of the crackle of tension which still simmered around them.

'Yes, I suppose we do if we are to be believed. Shall I arrange something this time?' Her voice distracted him from thinking of things he had little right to think about. The moment his lips had met hers something had changed, and although a public kiss was necessary, he had never meant it to be one so filled with such explosiveness as that lingering touch of lips to lips.

'Not this time.' He forced his mind to focus, not prepared to admit that he intended to test just how far and fast the news of their engagement was spreading. The elite of New York's restaurants were always able to accommodate those who moved in Bianca's high circles, and it was time to test if he was yet ranked among them. 'Just keep next Friday evening free.'

'Friday it is, then.' Her voice trailed after her, as did her perfume, as she left the elevator. For a moment he watched, bewitched by the sway of her hips, encased in emerald green silk.

Following her, he shook his head and blinked. He had to stop wondering what really dating

Bianca Di Sione would be like. If he didn't, his whole plan, one that had taken years to come to fruition, was at stake. And he couldn't let that happen.

As a teenager living rough on the streets of St Petersburg, he'd vowed he would do all it took to seek revenge for his parents, for the life together they should have had, and if it hadn't been for the underhand dealings of ICE, he wouldn't need Bianca to gain him acceptance into any society.

If it hadn't been for ICE, he wouldn't have been forced to steal just to feed himself and the other poor urchins he'd met while living rough. He wouldn't have been caught and sent to the youth prison camps, hidden away in the country. The gruelling years he'd spent there had made him a man before his time and now that man was ready to exact payment. So what if the delectable Bianca Di Sione was part of it.

'Goodnight, Liev.' Her voice pierced the past he'd slipped into and he quickly focused his attention on the woman who stood before him.

'Goodnight, Bianca.' He lifted her fingertips to his lips and kissed them gently. 'Until next Friday.'

Before he could do anything else, he turned and marched away, because if he didn't he was in danger of giving everything away by either allowing the past to get the better of him and demanding answers from her about the company her brother now headed, or by giving into the urge to kiss her—really kiss her.

CHAPTER FIVE

THE FOLLOWING FRIDAY Bianca sat at the intimate candlelit table of one of New York's most exclusive restaurants and looked out at the unrivalled view of the city. If Liev had been able to secure such a table at short notice, she knew that word of their engagement was spreading through society.

Not only was it spreading through society. It was spreading through her family and she was ashamed to say that she hadn't yet been able to tell them herself, as if by not doing so made it less of a lie.

She'd first had a call from Matteo and had hated that she'd had to deceive her older brother, telling him she was so happy, that she'd met the man of her dreams and hadn't wanted to wait a moment longer. He had been sceptical, questioning her, and that had almost pushed her to tell the truth. But how could she say she was being blackmailed—for a bracelet?

Then calls from some of the others had followed and she had been forced to tell the lie over and over. She also agreed that once Dario's launch was over they could all get together and meet the man who'd swept her off her feet. Except by then she would be nearing the end of her ridiculous deal with Liev Dragunov and hoped she would be able to stall them until she got the bracelet back. Once it was all over she could tell them she'd made a mistake, because under no circumstances did she want any of her family to know just what she was doing for her grandfather until she had the bracelet. She couldn't risk Liev taking it back to Russia, not when it meant so much to her grandfather.

'I'm impressed.' She turned her attention from the view to the man opposite. The angles of Liev's face, which had once made him look hard and unyielding, now made him appear more handsome. Or was it because he was actually smiling?

'With our engagement making the headlines this week, there was no question of not getting a table at any of New York's finest restaurants. It was, of course, a test to see just how far being engaged to you has brought me.' His voice held a new lightness to it but she couldn't relax.

She couldn't afford to, not when he'd been on her mind all week, lingering on the edge of her thoughts as she worked on Dario's forthcoming launch. When she'd opened a file for Liev, and had begun filling in the few details she'd overheard on their first date, she realised she knew very little else about him and checked again on the internet to find nothing much existed. There was nothing about his family, his education or his love life. Nothing. As if he'd never existed before he arrived in New York.

'And are you happy with the progress so far?' She watched the champagne bubble up in her glass, unable to maintain eye contact with him because of the whispers of awareness which brushed over her. They reminded her of how it had felt to be kissed by him and how much she'd wanted that kiss to continue.

'It is a start, but not yet enough.' His sharp words forced her to look again at him. His tailored suit showed off his physique, giving him a razor-sharp business look she couldn't help but admire. It was also blatantly obvious he wasn't going to settle for anything less than he wanted.

'We now need to begin planning your launch, which means I need to know a little more about you.' She kept her tone as businesslike as she could, but with those grey eyes watching her so intently, it was almost impossible. Shyness began to creep over her. Something she hadn't shown publicly for many years, preferring to hide behind a hardened mask of professionalism for which she was renowned. She was also well aware that she was referred to as the ice princess and had seen the gossip columns all week speculating if Liev was the man to melt that heart.

If only they knew the truth.

'Is that something we should be doing on a date?' His suggestive smile as he sat back to allow their first course to be placed on the table sent nerves skittering down her spine, closely followed by a tingle of awareness. Was that because he'd called tonight a date or because he'd smiled at her?

'I need to know more about you and, if you recall, we are not dating. We merely have an agreement. One I would prefer to think of as business—unless you'd like to use the more unsavoury term of *blackmail*?' She couldn't quite keep the tartness from her voice. Saying it aloud reminded her of the anger that she was allowing him to do this to her, making her feel as insignificant as she had that night of the prom.

'Very well. What do you need to know?' The smile had left his lips and his eyes now glittered with barely concealed mistrust, confirming he was hiding something or that his reasons for demanding the three-month engagement were not what he'd led her to believe.

'You mentioned at the charity dinner last week that you built your business up from nothing. That must have taken some doing and it's something I can use. But I need to know more.' Her business mind was beginning to take over, to leave the timid and vulnerable Bianca in the shadows, where she belonged.

Creating an image for her clients was what she was good at, and right now, keeping things on a more professional level was far more comfortable than the simmering tension which arced constantly between them, making her think again and again of that kiss.

'I was eighteen when we entered a new century and was determined to put my past behind me, so I started a computer repair business. I was self-taught and good at it. Those years with my father had served me well, and as you can see today, my company is very successful.'

'Self-taught?' She picked up on something she could use.

'My father was in the business and I grew up with computers as a big part of my childhood.'

'You must have missed your father. How old were you when he died?' She probed deeper, even though she sensed him shutting her out second by second, question by question.

'Twelve years old.'

Bianca recognised the fierce tone of his voice which covered up hurt. It was exactly what she did, but she also knew he wouldn't appreciate her saying she understood. How could any person understand what it was to lose a parent when you were young unless they, too, knew the pain? 'That must have been hard for you and your mother.'

'She died before my father. I had no one after he died.' Each word was clipped and short and her heart constricted for him.

She had lost both her parents, but as a two-year-old it didn't have such an immediate impact on her life, not when Allegra had stepped neatly into the role of mother and her grandfather had always been around. It must have been so much harder for Liev. She looked at him, imagining the young boy, alone and grieving.

'You were totally alone?' The whisper her voice had become revealed the sadness he'd evoked within her, bringing painful memories of her own to the surface.

He nodded slowly, the thin line of his lips showing the control he was using, and she knew she should stop, but with her heartstrings tugged by the thought of him alone in the world as a young boy, she couldn't.

'How and where did you live after your father died?' she asked, but seeing his jaw clench, she almost dreaded the answer. Surely he'd had some distant family who could have taken him in. Surely he hadn't been like those kids at the homeless shelter her business sponsored.

'I survived by doing whatever was necessary.' He was aiming to shock her. She could sense it in him, the way he sat, the way he looked at her, but she wasn't shocked. This man was a survivor, a born fighter, and she had the distinct impression that if everything were taken away from him right now, he would reinvent himself and become even more successful.

Liev had to stop thinking about Bianca like this, as if she was the woman he truly wanted to be with, the woman to share his past and build a future with. Each time she asked a question, she unlocked something inside him, prised open the door to his past a little more.

It was a door he'd slammed shut and locked years ago. He had to stop opening it now, stop her digging into his past, because she would find far more than she ever expected, far more than he wanted to reveal.

Instead of dwelling on what she might find, he steered the conversation the way he wanted it to go. 'I soon realised I had an aptitude for making money as well as working with computers. It wasn't long before I had my own premises and began selling my own software.'

'When did you begin selling globally?' Her attention was well and truly caught, and he found it a pleasurable change for a woman to be interested in what he did rather than how much money he made. He had met too many women like that lately and begrudgingly admitted that Bianca may not be quite as frivolous as he first thought, that perhaps she wasn't a carbon copy of the woman who'd broken his young and inexperienced heart, shattering it beyond repair.

But she wants the bracelet. Those words goaded him to reconsider.

Inwardly he breathed a sigh of relief. The questions she was asking were coming from Bianca the businesswoman. If they were coming from Bianca the woman, they would have led in a very different direction—somewhere he didn't go, not with anyone.

'Almost immediately. It was my aim from the very beginning.' That had always been his aim, more than that it had been to become so successful and wealthy that no other company could swallow him up, spitting him out and casting him aside, as had happened to his father.

'Was it something you had always wanted to do?'

'I always wanted to show the world I was a fighter, that whatever life threw at me I'd get back up, become more successful. I've gone from nothing to being able to buy whatever I want. I'm proud of that achievement.'

Everything he did, every deal he made, every new programme he produced and every office he opened around the world was for his parents, for what they should have had. Just as being here with Bianca was.

'That's very impressive. The press will love it.'

There was genuine warmth in her voice, but he ignored it, instantly on alert. 'The press don't need to know. I will not have my parents' names dragged up just to sell a product.'

Her eyes widened as she raised her brows in

question. 'A certain amount of your story will have to be told, but I understand about wanting to keep your parents out of it.'

'You more than most should.' He pushed his half-eaten starter away; his taste for fine dining had diminished rapidly. He might as well be eating stale bread again.

She reached out and touched his hand. 'And I do.'

Her dark eyes met his, their gazes locked and her hand remained over his, the warmth of it strangely comforting. This was a woman who did truly know the pain of growing up without parents. Although he'd bet she hadn't had to live rough and fight for every scrap of food that passed her lips.

She wouldn't have had to endure time in prison because of being forced to steal food, not just for herself but for other homeless kids, some much younger. She wouldn't have had to forge herself a new identity just to be able to shake off the past and make it in life afterwards. She'd had the cushion of a successful family business, something he could have had if it hadn't been for the underhand dealings of another business.

'Then you know it's not easy. You don't need the full details to appreciate that, and I'm sure with your ability to focus on what's important for a successful launch, you can leave them out.' He kept his tone firm and pulled his hand from beneath hers.

The look of hurt which rushed across her beautiful face, one less made up than the previous time they'd seen each other, snagged at his conscience. He shouldn't be so hard on her. She was only his key to gaining the revenge he'd first vowed on as he'd laboured in prison. She wasn't the ultimate goal.

'I won't focus on your past, but the present. It will be the press who will do that, which I'm afraid is all par for the course.' That tough mask of professionalism was back. For a moment he thought he'd seen real vulnerability in her eyes. 'And I have the perfect opportunity to show the world the man you are now. Leave it to me.'

'Do not forget, Bianca, that it is in your interests to keep negative press coverage at bay—if you want the bracelet.' Anger simmered at the thought of his past being exposed, something he'd lived constantly with, but for the first time, it mattered what someone else would think. It mattered what Bianca would think.

Never before had he cared what anyone had thought of him, and now the very woman he'd forced himself into close proximity with was making him care. He pushed the newfound emotion down and watched as she glared back at him.

'I will do whatever is necessary to get that bracelet back, Liev—including covering up your obviously dubious past and focusing on the good parts.' The words flew at him and only the waiter clearing away the first course halted the flow of those angry words.

He sat back and watched the sparks fly. He'd been waiting for the appearance of the fiery brunette who'd stood toe to toe with him at the auction house, all spitting fury and indignation. The woman who'd stirred the man within his toughened exterior.

So her focus was still on the bracelet. She wanted it back—and badly. Again he wondered at its significance.

'I'm pleased to hear it.' He wouldn't let her know yet that her guard had slipped, even if only briefly. He would have to do some more investigation on the silver bracelet which was now stored in his safe. Before he gave it back to her, he had to know why it was so important.

Bianca was saved from further humiliation by the arrival of their main course. As she ate, barely tasting the delicious food, she watched the amber sunset darkening and the lights of New York shining ever more vibrantly. She hadn't felt as unsure of herself as she was now for many years, and again she wished she could call Allegra and talk things through with her.

Not that that would help much, not now she'd given away the fact that she was prepared to do just about anything to get the bracelet back. She hadn't missed the slight narrowing of his icy grey eyes as she'd let those words slip out. He was shrewd and had already proved he was an almost unmovable force, one which would have to be reckoned with if she got in its way.

The best way forward was to keep everything on a strictly professional basis. 'What do you really want from me, Liev?' The words came out as fast as she'd thought of them, replacing what she'd intended to ask about his company and the software he was launching.

'As I have explained, I need acceptance into society and to do that I need you at my side.' He put down his cutlery, abandoning his food, and looked at her, the sharp glint in his eyes reminding her, if she needed it, just who she was dealing with. 'And, of course, I need your PR skills for my company.'

She was beginning to suspect there was

more to this than just what he'd told her. Those earlier doubts she'd had about him surfaced once more and she couldn't help but voice her questions. 'You should do more interviews, make yourself more accessible to the public. Why haven't you spoken to the press? I couldn't find anything online.'

'Because, unlike you, they will not be content to leave the past in the past, and I'm sure you, of all people, can understand the need not to bring up the deaths of my parents constantly.'

He was right about that, and for the moment she was prepared to give him the benefit. She put down her knife and fork, the meal now well and truly spoilt. 'The only way I can see to be able to move on from here is to be open about your past, but also create more speculation about our relationship.'

'Then I have exactly the invitation we need. Tomorrow evening we have been invited to a party.' He delivered the news to her and she frowned at him.

'I don't recall a party invite.'

'I had a phone call this morning from Margaret O'Neil. She mentioned she'd heard about our engagement and suggested we might like to attend her party.'

'That is good. Being a guest there will achieve just about all you have been wanting.' It would also mean she could possibly get the bracelet sooner and that could only be for the good with her grandfather's failing health. 'I'd like to go home now. I don't think anything more will be gained from being here like this. Maybe leaving before dessert will create more speculation.'

'Very clever. Passionate lovers abandon meal halfway through.' He lifted his brows and smiled at her in such a seductive way she caught her breath and held it against the thud of her pulse. Liev left some bills to settle the check and stood up. 'I will escort you home.'

Just as he had previously done, Liev walked Bianca to her door and she paused outside, beating back the strange urge to prolong talking with him. But what was she going to do? Invite him in for coffee?

'Goodnight, Liev,' she said softly as once again he lifted her fingertips to his lips. The heat that slid down her arm was more in keeping with a passionate romantic affair, not a blackmailed engagement. But she couldn't help it. Just being with him did something to her.

She watched him as her pulse continued to race. What was the matter with her? It was as if she was a teenager again, falling for the bad boy at high school, the one who would break her heart. She couldn't be falling for him—could she?

'Do you not wish we had met another way?' The velvety smoothness of his words made her skin tingle, as did their meaning.

'No—absolutely not,' she lied.

He laughed softly, his eyes warming and his expression full of undisguised charm. 'So hotly denied, but can it be true?'

She tried to pull her fingers from his hand, but he held her firmly. She had no choice other than look up into his face. 'It's true.'

'So if I kiss you right now, just as I did last week at the charity dinner, you will not respond with such undisguised desire?'

What was she doing, encouraging this conversation? But she couldn't help it, couldn't help wondering how he would kiss her this time.

'There is nobody to witness the kiss. What possible reason could you have now to kiss me?'

'Because you are a very beautiful woman, one who should be kissed.' He moved towards her, brushed his lips over hers, as if tasting them.

'No, Liev, this is not part of the deal.' She

kept her voice firm but couldn't help staying dangerously close to him.

'No, but admit it, Bianca. You want me to kiss you. You want me to melt that sleeping heart the gossip columns are all talking about.'

She put her hands firmly on his chest, ignoring the spark that flew from that contact. 'The only time I will kiss you is in public and then only because it is part of the role of being madly in love with you.'

'Are you sure, Bianca?' His voice was now a hoarse whisper that made her stomach flip and her heart race.

Before she had time to respond, he lowered his head, claimed her lips in a kiss that verged on demanding. Her head spun, and although she knew she shouldn't, she moved her lips against his, tasting the forbidden. Her fingers clutched the lapels of his jacket as he put his arms around her, pulling her close.

It was insane. It was also amazing.

'No.' She pushed against him and he pulled back but didn't let go of her. 'That can never happen again, not like that.'

He drew in a deep breath and let it go slowly, as if curbing an angry response. 'It will if we are in public. If it's part of your role, as you called it.'

'Just go,' she snapped, and relief and disappointment washed over her as he moved back from her. 'Go, Liev. This charade is over for tonight.'

'Until tomorrow, Bianca.'

With those words haunting her, she watched him stride back to the elevator, wondering what had just happened. Why had she taunted him, but more importantly, why had she kissed him?

It would not happen again.

CHAPTER SIX

BIANCA'S NERVES WERE almost frayed as she waited for Liev the next evening. She anticipated this would be their last public outing, but she'd arranged a publicity interview for him at the shelter, and together with tonight's photos appearing in the glossy celebrity magazines, she hoped he would be satisfied and have what he wanted. After the interview she fully intended that their engagement could become more low-key. The thought of spending more time with Liev was not something she relished, especially when he could provoke such new emotions in her.

She wasn't sure if their engagement would achieve the acceptance he wanted, something she still wasn't convinced of, but if they remained engaged, as far as everyone else was concerned, he could continue to pursue that himself, leaving her free to concentrate on Dario's forthcoming launch.

Her brothers and sisters were another matter entirely and she'd prepared herself for the onslaught of further questions from them. She had no idea what she'd say to her grandfather and hadn't bargained on the request from him to meet her fiancé. Just thinking of the lies she would have to tell made her nauseous. Grandfather deserved better than that—but he also deserved to be able to be reunited with the bracelet he'd owned when he arrived in New York all those years ago. That in itself was a story Bianca longed to hear more about, but first she had another *date* with her fiancé—and hopefully her last. After last night's kiss and her obvious loss of control, it would have to be.

Prompt as ever, Liev knocked on her apartment door and she took in a deep breath and prepared herself to spend the evening with a man who unsettled and intrigued her all at the same time. Until last night's kiss, she'd been beginning to enjoy his company and had found herself more relaxed, but she must never forget how he was blackmailing her. This was not an ordinary love affair and they could never be a normal couple.

She opened the door and drew in a sharp breath. Liev stood calmly waiting, dressed in a tuxedo which hugged his body, more than hinting at his latent strength and sending her wayward thoughts awry once more. His brow was furrowed into a frown, yet still he very definitely was the most striking man she'd ever met.

'Good evening, Bianca.'

She shivered as his gaze slid down her black silk dress, which skimmed the floor, neither concealing nor revealing. Shyness suddenly swept over her and she looked away from him as heat infused her body as hotly as her cheeks.

She had to ask him now. There was no way she was going to be able to spend the entire evening at his side and look relaxed and happy if she was worrying telling him about her grandfather's unexpected request.

'Before we go, I have two suggestions that will further this charade of yours hopefully to its goal.' She heard her voice, steady and matter-of-fact, and marvelled at her ability to be one thing when inside she was something else completely different.

'I'm intrigued.' He stepped closer to her and she trembled like a new leaf in the spring breeze as she looked up into his eyes, shocked to see his darken until they resembled slate, reminding her of that kiss last night. 'What could possibly achieve that? Another kiss? Perhaps I should kiss you at the party—really kiss you, like you wanted me to last night?'

'I—I wanted no such thing.' She stammered over her words, the thought of being kissed by him making her pulse race wildly. If that last kiss was anything to go by, to be really kissed would be amazing. She'd never been kissed until the world spun and her heart felt light. Quickly she pulled her attention back to the reason for doing all this. The bracelet. 'That was not what I had in mind though.'

He moved closer, so close she thought he was going to kiss her right there and then. She breathed in and inhaled his newly applied aftershave, exotically spiced and incredibly heady. She looked up, holding his gaze, trying for bold and confident, but all she could manage was a startled gasp as he brushed his fingers over her cheek.

The heat of that light touch seared her skin, but she couldn't move away even when she knew she should. Every loving look, every caressing touch, was all an act. She was well aware of that, but it made her think of the love letter she'd found as a child tucked away between the pages of a book in the family library. One she'd read again and again over the years, each time wishing she, too, could find such a powerful love.

What was between her and Liev was not love. There was attraction, at least for her, but for him it was only a deal. A means to an end. Nothing more.

'That is a shame. You were made to be kissed.' His voice had deepened and his accent became so strong she could barely understand what he said.

How could she be made to be kissed when she'd hardly experienced more than a light touch on the cheek? Last night's kiss had been a new experience, one that could distract her if she allowed it.

The night of her prom rushed back at her. She'd wanted to be kissed then, too, wanted to be loved. She'd thought she'd found her true love, but fate had dealt her a cruel hand. That disastrous night had set the precedence for the following ten years—never, ever, allow a man close enough to hurt her again.

She'd thought she'd got it covered, that she was immune to the charms that seemed to penetrate even the toughest women. Her mask was deep and strong, but now a man who had proved from the outset he was using her was chipping away at that mask—unveiling the real

Bianca layer by layer. She couldn't let it happen. If he saw beneath the veneer she lived behind, she would be lost, unable to guard her heart from the pain of being used—yet again.

'I was most certainly not.' Her indignant tone made him step back, but there was a flicker of amusement in his eyes, irritating her further. 'And most definitely not by you.'

'That's not how it seemed last night.'

'Last night was a mistake. The only way I would ever kiss you again is if it was necessary for this facade of an engagement. Nothing you can say or do will change my mind.'

'Is that a challenge?'

'You are insufferable.' She flung the words back at him, outraged that he'd used her response last night against her. 'It would be far more productive if we visit my family home. It's sure to be noticed and make it into the celebrity columns.'

'Very clever.' The way he was looking at her sent butterflies charging wildly around her stomach, despite the building humiliation at his overconfident flirtation.

'I've also lined up an interview with a top New York magazine, so you can tell of your past rather than the press dig it up.'

'You really are excelling yourself. When is the interview?'

'Tomorrow afternoon. Then I thought we could visit my family home next weekend, use that as a bit more engagement publicity.'

'I will be at the interview tomorrow, but we will not visit your grandfather next weekend. I have a long weekend away planned for us. I have invited one of the magazines for a photo-shoot, giving them an engagement exclusive.'

Bianca's head was spinning. That wasn't what she'd meant at all. All she'd wanted was to set her grandfather's mind at rest. How did he manage to turn everything to his advantage?

'I'm not sure that's such a good idea,' she said anxiously, wondering what her family would think when they saw such a piece, let alone the fact that she'd always strived to be out of the limelight.

'It is not negotiable, Bianca. It is all arranged. We will visit your grandfather as we return to New York. If I meet him in person before the article goes out, I'm sure that will settle your worries.'

Worries? Was that what he thought of them as? It was all right for him; he didn't care about deceiving anyone. He didn't have any family to worry about. The fact that she was lying to her brothers and sisters was one thing, but lying to an old man, one whose life was ebbing away far too fast, was not something she was happy with.

It hurt to think that she'd take Liev to meet him, pretend to be head over heels in love just to reassure her grandfather, then upset him, giving him more to worry about when she broke it off.

'A weekend away and an engagement photoshoot aren't necessary.'

'It is if you want your bracelet before the end of three months.'

'But it's too intimate, too…' Again she floundered for words.

'It is publicity, Bianca, the sort that will achieve my aims quickly.'

'I see that, once again, you have made sure I have no option but to play this your way.' The sharpness of her tone made his brows rise. 'Again you are all but blackmailing me.'

'No, an exclusive like this was always part of the deal. Meeting with your grandfather, however, was not.' He moved towards her and his tone softened. 'But I am not as mercenary as you like to believe, so we will visit him.'

Bianca was baffled by his sudden change of

mood and blinked in shock as his closeness invaded her senses once more. How could she be so attracted to, so drawn by, the very man who had such power over her? Not for the first time she wished tonight's party was already over.

Liev couldn't help but take in Bianca as she looked up at him, all wide-eyed. Her dark eye make-up and deep red lipstick was back and the black silk dress clung to her like a second skin. Diamonds sparkled from her ears and around her throat, and his ring shone on her finger. She was stunning, but he was also glimpsing someone softer, someone much more vulnerable beneath.

He brushed his fingers over her face once more and wondered if he wiped away the make-up would he reveal the true Bianca so easily. He doubted it, but talking about her grandfather had certainly made the mask slip.

She'd also agreed to the perfect opportunity to show the world they were a couple. It was far more than he'd hoped for, far more than he'd ever imagined as he'd snatched her precious bracelet from under her nose, and exactly what he needed.

Time away from everyone and everything would give him the perfect opportunity to find out all he needed to know about Dario Di Sione and ICE—and use their engagement in the most public way possible.

'So you would have no objection to our official engagement photographs being taken?'

'No.' She looked at him sceptically and he could see the shadow of doubt in her eyes. 'We should be at the party now.'

He offered her his arm, enjoying the feeling of her close to him. The heightened response of his body to that closeness was more pronounced than he'd yet experienced. Bianca Di Sione was getting to him, infiltrating the barriers he'd erected as an angry twelve-year-old to keep out tender emotions. The only consolation was that she, too, was losing her fiery edge, that harshness she hid behind which was more than the make-up she wore. She was as aware of him as he was of her.

That awareness still sizzled through him as they arrived at the party. As with any high-society event, the press were waiting outside the hotel for an opportune shot. The lenses clicked and the flashguns burst into life around them as he guided Bianca into the hotel.

Ever the professional, she smiled, pausing briefly for the press, her body melding against his as a lover's would, pushing his limits of restraint ever higher.

The earlier shock of realisation that he enjoyed being with her, enjoyed the feel of her body close to his, surfaced once more. Contrary to all he'd previously expected, he actually looked forward to a whole weekend at his island retreat. Once the exclusive interview on their engagement was over they would be alone. Nothing could get in the way of him finding out what he needed to know, and more importantly, she wouldn't be able to run home and hide.

'The guest list is large and very influential,' she said as they left the press behind for the peace of the hotel lobby. 'I will be able to make good connections for you this evening.'

Her voice pulled him out of his thoughts and back to the party, but his response was silenced as she let her wrap slide from her shoulders. Her strapless dress drew his attention and all he could think of was pressing his lips against the paleness of her shoulders.

'Nothing more than I would have expected from you.' Finally he managed to string a sentence together.

'I will take that as a compliment.' She smiled up at him. A real smile. One that made those beautiful lips appear even more kissable. Her eyes sparkled with genuine amusement and something happened as his pulse seemed to race. In that moment all he wanted to do was make her smile, to see the woman who lurked unexpectedly close to the surface of that tough exterior she literally painted on.

'Not only are you very talented, but you look even more beautiful this evening.'

She blushed and looked away from him. A sense of satisfaction filled him as he realised that whatever it was between them, it was enabling him to see a far softer side to her than he suspected she wanted him to see.

She turned and walked away, taking a glass of champagne as she entered the party, giving him no option but to follow.

As Liev placed his hand in the small of her back, Bianca pinned a smile on her face, ever the professional role player. The light touch made her skin sizzle and for a moment she couldn't look at him, knowing the heat of awareness to his every move had suffused her cheeks.

Just as at previous evenings, she felt all eyes on them and could imagine what the whispered conversations would be about. It showcased everything about society she disliked and everything Liev was determined to acquaint himself with. She had to hang on to why she was doing this, that the reason for flaunting herself so blatantly with him among them was her grandfather.

'We have already gained their attention,' Liev whispered close to her ear, too close, and she couldn't help the shiver of pleasure as his breath caressed her skin.

She swallowed hard, determined to keep her smile in place. 'Going away may not be necessary after tonight.'

He reached out and pushed her hair back from her face, his fingers skimming her bare shoulder as he did so. 'Don't you want to be alone with me?' His voice was low and a hint of something very seductive lingered in it.

'I do have other clients,' she retorted quickly, a little too quickly if the quirk of his brow was anything to go by.

'But only one fiancé.'

Before she had time to say anything, his fingers had taken her chin, lifting it up, and she knew he was going to kiss her. Every buzzing nerve in her body anticipated it. He pressed his lips against hers and instantly she responded, despite her resolve to merely role-play.

'Very good, Bianca,' he murmured against them, sending sparks of heat firing through her.

She drew in a deep breath and stepped back, away from the warmth of his body, realising nothing had made her stay there except his gentle hold on her chin—and the burning need to experience his kiss again.

'Role play.' She flashed him a smile and turned to greet their hostess, who was making her way over to them. 'Margaret, how lovely to see you. This is my fiancé, Liev Dragunov. Liev, this is Margaret O'Neil. Our families go back a long way.'

'Enchanted.' Liev's charm worked wonders on Margaret, known for her intolerance of self-made newcomers. If she was convinced, then the rest of New York society would soon follow. Her job was almost over. Tomorrow's interview would clinch that. So why did that fill her with a strange sense of loss?

Liev could sense the underlying bristle of the older lady and turned his charm up, but he didn't miss the small frown which furrowed Bianca's face so briefly. He bowed his head in recognition of her obvious high place in society, adhering to all the protocol he had no wish to be governed by once he had what he wanted.

'I am having a summer ball next month. You must come along and bring this delightful fiancé of yours, Bianca. I absolutely insist.'

'We would be honoured to attend.' He gave her the full force of his smile, knowing exactly the effect it had on women, and then turned it on Bianca, satisfied by her lost-for-words look.

Other guests caught Margaret's attention and she excused herself, leaving him and Bianca once more alone in a room full of people he had no real intention of befriending.

'It seems we will be mixing in high circles next month.' He took two fresh flutes of champagne from a passing waiter and handed one to Bianca. She took it with a glimmer of suspicion in her eyes. 'To success.'

'Success?' She glanced at him from beneath her lashes, the coy look doing untold things to his already frustrated libido. Since when did he go in for such games as that? Never. If he wanted something, including women, he got it. Bianca had not been on his wanted list, but somehow she was now there, right at the top and clashing with his almost lifelong desire to avenge his family and expose ICE.

'Do you not want success, Bianca? Do you not want the bracelet you so obviously covet?'

She moved against him, catlike in the way

her body seemed to curl against his, pushing his wayward thoughts further over the edge. If she wasn't careful she'd find herself being marched from the room to somewhere private where they could finish what she was so very intentionally starting.

'In some ways we are very similar,' she said softly, and he watched as she paused to sip the champagne. 'You will stop at nothing to get what you want—but remember, Liev, neither will I.'

He caught hold of her chin, more firmly than he'd done before, and watched as her eyes darkened to that sexy deep blue. He brushed his lips over hers, enjoying the exhilarating challenge she offered. 'I will remember that.'

CHAPTER SEVEN

BIANCA COULDN'T HELP but feel pleased as the
party drew to a close in the small hours. She
and Liev had been in demand much of the evening. Her job was almost done, which would
mean very soon their engagement could be
dropped. She'd get the bracelet and he would
have the acceptance he required. She wouldn't
have to spend such evenings with the man
who'd turned her into the kind of woman she'd
never imagined she could be.

She enjoyed sparring with him, and the
thought of not seeing much more of Liev sad-
dened her. He'd infiltrated her life, become
a part of it, filling her mind when he wasn't
around and infusing her body with a kind of
awareness she was beginning to accept came
from being with a man she was genuinely attracted to. Although there could be no future
in such notions, not after the way he'd used

her, and that was something she had to keep in her mind to prevent those fairy-tale ideas of love getting a hold.

She didn't try to persuade Liev that he didn't need to walk her to her door as he had done on each of their previous dates. It might be the early hours of the morning, but she wasn't ready to say goodnight yet. Being with him was becoming comfortable, perhaps a little too comfortable.

As she stopped outside her front door, key in hand, she looked up at him. It was as if her resistance was lowering, cast aside by a man she found infuriating and attractive.

'I've enjoyed this evening.' Were those soft words really from her?

His eyes, suddenly much darker, searched her face. 'As have I.'

Before she could understand what was happening, he'd brushed stray hair from her face. The heat of his fingers on her skin made her pulse leap wildly, but she couldn't do anything. She was being drawn in by a sensation so new, so intense, she was powerless to resist.

He spoke in Russian, his voice husky as he moved closer to her, their bodies almost touching. She had no idea what he'd said. All she knew was that he was going to kiss her.

Every instinct in her body told her that. And she wanted him to.

'Liev,' she whispered as his lips brushed briefly against hers, testing her reaction, her acceptance.

'We are still in public and you are not yet in the safety of your apartment, so your role still needs to be played. Besides, I want to kiss you, Bianca. Really kiss you.'

Her body hummed with anticipation and tingled with warmth. He desired her. He wanted her not because it was part of the deal or part of the show they had to put on, but because he wanted *her*.

Could she trust him? Could she trust herself? Last night's encounter at this very door told her she couldn't trust him—or herself.

'It will only complicate things.' She forced herself away, to turn and put her key in the door and open it, hoping he would leave.

'Only if we allow it to.' His breathing seemed deeper and the image he created as he stood there in the glory of that after-party look twisted her heart and she knew it was already too late. For her, at least, things were already complicated.

'Bianca, can you honestly deny there is

something between us? Something that needs exploring?'

'I can't.' She backed away from him, into the safety of her apartment. She should just close the door on him, but she couldn't. That would be like shutting herself away and she was tired of doing that. Tired of looking for the hidden agenda each time a man paid her a compliment.

'But you want to.' Those husky tones sent a shiver down her spine, a tremor of anticipation.

'Yes.' She couldn't help herself any more—not after what she'd sampled last night.

She'd never known what it was like to be kissed, really kissed, as he'd said. She could see the raw desire in his eyes and it terrified her, in an exciting kind of way. But still that night of her prom haunted her.

'But I can't.' She stepped back into her apartment and he came in after her. She'd as good as invited him in.

'Can't or won't?'

'I won't. We are not in a relationship. This is just a deal, Liev, and only requires perfunctory kisses in public. It does not warrant behind-closed-doors passion.'

For a moment, she thought she saw him

flinch, but she had to bring their deal into it. If only to remind him of what she'd claimed last night and to remind herself this wasn't what she wanted—or needed.

'My apologies.' His words were velvet smooth but still that sizzle burned in his eyes. 'You are so very beautiful, it is hard to remember the terms of our agreement.'

Now it was her turn to flinch. He was reminding her of his power over her—and it had nothing to do with their deal and everything to do with the man himself. 'You may have blackmailed me in order to get me to represent your company and the acceptance from society you crave, but you will never have anything more of me.'

'Ah, I see. Saving yourself for Mr Right?' His words were light and flirtatious, not a hint of anything that suggested any kind of malice. But what he'd said had struck a chord. What would he say if he knew she was a virgin, that she had hardly been kissed? What would he do if she told him just how much she wanted to be kissed by him? A real kiss.

'Something like that, yes.' She couldn't help but goad him as embarrassment made her brash, and was rewarded with the surprised rise of his brows. 'Goodnight, Liev.'

* * *

As Liev got out of the taxi the next afternoon, he wondered if he had the right address. Everything about the neighbourhood brought back his past. Then he saw Bianca, looking like a flower in the desert as she walked towards him.

'Why are we here?' he asked, trying to ignore the fire of desire which rushed through him just from seeing her as it mixed with thoughts of his own youth in an area not dissimilar to this deprived street.

'The interview.' Her delicate brows drew together and she looked at him suspiciously. 'I've arranged for it to happen here at the shelter.'

'Shelter?' This was all getting too close to his past for comfort. Had she any idea what she was doing? What she was unlocking and forcing him to face?

'Yes. Bluebird Family Shelter.'

Anger brewed furiously. She really was intent on bringing out his past and exposing it to the world. He was about to tell her no, that this was a mistake, when a young man joined them.

'Good of you to agree to this, Mr Dragunov. I'm Nick. I run the shelter.'

Liev shook his hand. There was no way out now and he consoled himself that by doing this he'd be highlighting the plight of youngsters without homes. 'My pleasure.'

'Great. Let's go and meet some of the lads.'

Aware they were also promoting their engagement, Liev took Bianca's hand and followed Nick inside the graffiti-covered walls, his past rushing back at him.

'Afternoon, Miss B,' one youth said as they walked through the building to a small walled area outside at the back of the tall brick building, which reminded Liev of a prison.

'Afternoon.'

For a moment Liev was too stunned by where he was to notice the respect in the lad's voice and the warmth of Bianca's as she'd replied. Was this one of her frequently used interview locations?

More of the youngsters greeted her, most regarding him with suspicion. 'You seem to be well known here.'

'Supporting this place has been my personal project for over ten years.' She looked up at him as they stood in the high-walled courtyard, with the sounds of New York City drifting in. 'I grew up with privileges, well aware that many didn't.'

'Without Miss Di Sione's help, this place would have closed long ago,' added Nick, and he called over a teenage lad.

Bianca did this? Supported these kids and their families? He looked at her and saw her cheeks colour beneath his scrutiny. He was about to say something when the lad Nick had called over approached. He nodded in a way that showed his respect for her but didn't damage his toughened exterior. Then he glanced at him and the years fell away. It was like looking at himself twenty years ago.

'Great to meet you. I'm Liev.' He didn't offer to shake hands. He knew well enough how much personal space was valued. The lad nodded solemnly and Liev wished he could reach him, tell him he knew how he felt.

'Billy will stand with you for a photo,' offered Nick.

'Just one.' Billy spoke and finally made eye contact with him. As he looked into the eyes of his youth, he could feel the warmth of Bianca's presence, keeping him from sliding back to the nightmare of those days.

'Billy's been here on and off with his family for three years,' said Bianca softly. 'Just one photo is all we need, Billy. Thanks.'

Bianca watched as the photographer took the photo, cajoling Billy to pose for at least one more. Then the interviewer asked them questions and Billy slipped away, melting effortlessly into the background. She could feel each question making Liev more tense, more closed off.

The next question was fired at him. 'You haven't had a good childhood yourself, I understand?'

She saw Liev glance at Billy, where he lingered in the shadows, as if he'd forgotten everything else, and Bianca's heart reached out to Liev and the boy he had once been. A boy just like Billy.

'I was twelve when my parents died. They'd lost everything in a bad business deal and I had nobody, no choice but to live on the streets of St Petersburg.'

Billy stepped back out of the shadows and looked at Liev, making eye contact, which this time seemed full of healthy respect.

'How did you get where you are now?' the interviewer asked, obviously intrigued by the connection between Liev and the boy. Just as she was.

'I did anything I could.'

Billy nodded at this, approving of what he was hearing. Bianca wanted to know more, but sensed Liev's caution. This was an interview, after all, and she didn't want him baring his soul, giving away his deepest secrets. She would have to find another way to discover what really lay behind that comment, because right now she wanted nothing more than to protect his past.

'I'd have given anything for a place like this,' Liev continued, but she could hear the caution in his tone. 'The place I stayed in for five years was much tougher.'

Bianca was aware of notes being made. She'd thought bringing him here would be good, that she'd be able to play on the bad-boy-makes-good image the press loved, but right now she felt as if she'd lost Liev to that past.

'Thank you, gentlemen,' she cut in efficiently, ending the interview. 'I think you have enough now.'

Billy had gone. Disappeared from sight. Was that how Liev had lived? Was that why she couldn't find out anything about him?

Liev turned to look at her, his eyes harder than she'd ever seen them before. She met his gaze, matching his fury. This was exactly the sort of promotion that would achieve all the open doors he craved. Had he really expected to keep everything he'd ever done quiet and away from prying eyes?

'You should have warned me what today

was all about.' His words were gentle enough, but she didn't miss the sharp edge to them.

'What did you expect, Liev? More red-carpet shots? That's not the way to the hearts of New York society.' The brittle edge to her response was born out of disappointment and despair. She really needed that bracelet, and the sooner, the better. She pinned all her hopes on this interview. This was exactly the right thing, but somehow it had softened her heart even more to him. She'd seen something raw and profound within him as he'd spoken, all the while looking at Billy.

'I said I didn't want my past used.'

'This is my personal charity, Liev, and the interview you've just given will benefit Billy and all the other kids here as much as you.'

Liev was seeing a new side to Bianca, one that banished his first impression of her being a spoilt princess firmly from his mind. Her motives for helping him, just for a bracelet, didn't add up, but he'd get to the bottom of that whilst they were away.

She intrigued him and he wanted to know more. Much more.

'You surprise me,' he said, trying to rein in his thoughts.

'Because I'm not the spoilt little rich girl you thought I was?' The spike of fury in her words was clear, as was the glitter of anger in her eyes.

'There's more to you than you let people know and I hope that over the next weekend we will both get to know one another better.'

'You make it sound as if it's more...' He saw her hesitancy in her face. 'Like a lovers' holiday.'

'That is exactly what it is supposed to appear, and if you get it right, Bianca, and the engagement exclusive works, it could be the last time you will have to endure my company.'

'It will work,' she said firmly. 'Email me the details.'

CHAPTER EIGHT

BIANCA WAS STILL reeling with the shock over Liev's romantic getaway plans as the yacht arrived at a private island in the Bahamas. Not only had he set up the exclusive interview and photoshoot, but he'd whisked her away to the most romantic setting of white sands, blue sea and endless sunshine. A lovers' paradise, one that should feel as good as a prison, trapping her with him and the ever-increasing desire she felt for him. It could be the warmth of the sun, or the relaxing time on the yacht along with champagne, but she didn't feel that in the least.

'How did you manage to set this up?' She took the hand he offered her and stepped onto the wooden jetty, glad she could hide her shock behind sunglasses. 'And find this idyllic setting?'

'With all the current interest in our engagement, an exclusive wasn't hard to negotiate, especially when I invited them to my secluded island home.' The drawl of his voice was soft and incredibly sexy and she wondered if the sun had already gone to her head; then what he actually said finally registered.

'Your island?'

'Is that something you hadn't found out about me, Bianca?' He didn't let her hand go. Instead he pulled her closer and she went willingly, moving so close until she was almost pressing herself against his body. 'Maybe being here will allow us both to discover more about each other.'

'Not with a magazine shoot going on.' She laughed softly, hardly able to understand just how she already felt so relaxed being here with him. What would it be like if they were here for no other reason than to get to know one another? The thought sent a sizzle of excitement zipping around her and she sighed in relief knowing that photographers and their assistants would invade any peace they had, that they wouldn't be as alone as it first appeared.

'That is not happening until Saturday morning.' He looked intently into her eyes and she almost forgot herself, almost melted completely against him.

'Saturday morning! But it's only Friday now. We can't stay here alone together until then.'

'We can and we will.' He took her sunglasses from her face and she just let him. 'I like to see your eyes, to see your thoughts in them, and right now, I see panic. But I promise you, Bianca, apart from playing your role at the photoshoot, nothing will happen here between us—unless you want it to.'

'So why hide away here for several days?'

'Bianca, do you really need to ask? The magazine will feel as if they have been invited into our own private love affair, able to glimpse the love we have for one another. It will also give us time to perfect that loving couple moment they will be expecting.'

Deep down she knew he was right. It would be exactly what the magazine readers would most want to see. But two days here, alone with a man who was unlocking a Bianca she never knew existed, was not a prospect she relished. But he had said nothing would happen that she didn't want.

'You're right,' she said, and she pulled her hand free of his and took back the sunglasses he held out to her. 'We'll do it your way.'

'The villa is this way.' Before she could say anything, he'd taken her hand and was walking along the wooden jetty which spanned across crystal blue waters towards the white sands, fringed by palm trees and lush green plants which shielded the villa from view.

Again that sizzle of anticipation raced through her. Two days alone with Liev. But would that be enough to get to know the real man? He led her along a pathway through the palm trees and she caught the first glimpse of the villa. It wasn't as big as she'd first imagined; in fact, it was small to the point of being cosy and nestled in the palm trees. Beyond it she could see the ocean. It was so romantic, exactly the kind of place she could imagine the lovers from the letter she'd found when she was younger coming to.

The coolness of the interior was welcoming as they entered. It was furnished more traditionally than she'd ever have imagined a man like Liev wanting, but to her it was simply perfect.

'It's such a beautiful home.' He let her hand go and she wandered to the windows and looked out over the ocean, its sparkling waters looking so inviting. She hadn't swum in the sea for so long.

'I'll show you to your room and then we can take a walk on the beach, maybe even a swim.'

He stood in the doorway, his casual clothes suiting him as much as the tuxedo he'd worn for the party. She didn't miss the mention of her room and relaxed. He obviously intended to keep his word. Nothing would happen if she didn't want it to. The problem was, she wanted it to.

'A walk would be nice, but I haven't come prepared for swimming.' She regretted that he hadn't given her more information when he'd told her they would be away for the weekend. The thought of a swim in the ocean was very enticing.

He walked from the living area and she followed him into a lovely and bright bedroom with doors which opened out onto a small shady garden and the beach beyond, basking in the afternoon sun. He picked up a package from the bed and turned to her.

'This might help.' His voice had deepened and his accent had become more pronounced, but his expression had softened, as if being in the sunshine was stripping away the hardness she'd become accustomed to.

Her eyes met his and she scanned them for any hint of what it might help with, but as she took the neatly gift-wrapped box from him,

she guessed what was inside the package.
'Thank you.'

She was stunned by this thoughtful gesture.
It was one she hadn't believed a man as ruthless as Liev would be capable of. It would,
though, make a swim more intimate, when she
was wearing his choice of swimwear.

'I'll meet you outside when you are ready.'
Before she could say any more, he left, closing the door to her room behind him. Never
had a man bought her a present, and unable to
contain her curiosity, she pulled the red bow
undone and opened the flat box. Inside was
a red bikini and the most delicately beautiful
cover-up she'd ever seen.

She blushed until her cheeks matched the
bikini at the thought of wearing it in front of
him, but she would look incredibly prudish and
ungrateful if she stayed in the summer dress
she was wearing. Besides, a swim in the sea
was becoming ever more inviting.

Liev watched as Bianca moved out onto the
terrace, pleased to see she'd accepted his gift.
The sheer red chiffon cover-up wasn't really
doing its job and he could see her soft curves
as the warm wind pressed the fabric against
her skin. She looked uncomfortable and vul-

nerable with her face almost free of make-up and her hair pulled up into a haphazard chignon which left some dangling sexily around her face.

'Red suits you,' he said as she walked towards him and was rewarded with a slight flush to her cheeks. In fact, red suited her too much.

'Swimwear is another look you wear well,' she said with that impish smile he'd seen briefly before. So she wasn't immune to him and neither was she embarrassed by him standing waiting for her in his swimming trunks and white shirt open. Was he finally beginning to melt the ice princess?

'If we walk a little first, there is a nice sheltered cove, perfect for swimming.'

As she fell into step beside him, he remained silent, waiting for her to decide the topic of conversation, hoping that eventually it would come round to what he wanted to know about her brother and ICE. By playing it cool, he hoped to lure her into lowering all those barriers she had up against the world and him in particular.

'How long have you had this place?' She looked out at the ocean as they strolled along and he couldn't resist taking in her long legs as she walked in the edge of the surf. The pull of attraction was becoming much stronger and harder to resist, just as it had each time he'd seen her, especially after the revelations of a much softer and caring Bianca at the shelter. On the way to the island there had been moments when he thought she felt the same way and his original plan of nothing ever happening between them was paling into insignificance.

He wanted her, more than he'd wanted any woman. At the same time he resented her more than any other woman. She was the spoilt little rich girl, pandered to and pampered with every luxury. But that opinion had changed. Or was it his increasing desire for her that changed it?

'I bought it last year but haven't yet put my mark on it.' An island paradise had been something his parents had talked of wanting. A place to escape the harshness of Russian winters. He'd achieved that for them, but had much more to do yet.

'I like it just the way it is.' She looked at him, her sunglasses shielding her eyes, hiding her thoughts, but it couldn't hide the relaxed smile or the genuine interest in her voice.

'This is the best place to swim,' he said, wanting to change the subject and give his mind and body something other than Bianca to focus on. He pulled off his shirt, dropped it to the warm sand and waded into the water. When he was waist-high in the ocean, he turned to look at her.

She was removing the cover-up and placing it on the sand next to his shirt along with her sunglasses. The thought of their clothes lying together on the beach only increased the throb of desire which coursed through him.

He smiled when she backed away a little as the waves came towards her. She was truly beautiful. Everything about her was perfect and he wanted to hold her against his body, feel her skin against his skin as he claimed her as his, even if it was to be only for a few days. He was under no illusions they could have anything else, not after the way they met.

'Don't be shy. Come on in. The water is great,' he called above the gentle rush of the waves and laughed as she dropped down and covered her body in water before standing up again, water running off her curves, stirring the rising passion within him higher still.

With a smile that lit up her face, she lowered herself into the water and started swimming to the platform, her strong strokes taking her quickly past him and away. He swam after her, reaching the platform at the same time. Her face was alive with vitality and excitement as he looked into her eyes and all he wanted to do was kiss her.

He moved forward in the water and saw her blue eyes widen, but she didn't move, didn't say anything. Before he could think what he was doing and why, his lips were on hers, tasting the salty water and the woman herself. Instantly she responded, her lips moving against his, and he cursed the fact they were holding on to a platform in the ocean. Seducing her had never been part of the plan. He'd even gone as far as telling her nothing would happen between them unless she wanted it.

He drew in a sharp breath of shock as she pushed herself against him and away. She called over her shoulder as her strokes began to pull her through the water. 'Race you back.'

He let her swim a few more strokes before pushing off, quickly catching up with her. He held back, keeping at least several strokes behind as she swam. As she reached the beach she began to run through the water and then flopped down at the edge, the waves lapping gently around her.

He joined her, sitting close and enjoying the feeling of the warm water over his legs. 'You are a good swimmer.' He had to force himself to talk of something neutral because all he wanted to do was kiss her—and not stop until he'd set light to the passion he knew was inside her too.

'I haven't swum for so long and certainly not in the ocean. I'd forgotten how liberating it can feel.' She put her arms out behind her and leant back, her face upturned to the sun, and inwardly he groaned as that throb of desire in him intensified, calling for satisfaction that only this woman could bring.

She hadn't mentioned the kiss, hadn't told him it wasn't what she wanted. If anything, she was flirting with him, taunting him with her body.

'Bianca.' His voice was decidedly husky as he said her name and she looked at him and he knew he'd finally found the real Bianca, the woman beneath that ice-princess exterior she liked the world to see.

She didn't answer, but slowly she moved towards him and he knew she wanted to be kissed as much as he wanted to kiss her. If he did kiss her now, he didn't know if he would be able to stop, didn't know if he could just switch off the ever-increasing desire for her.

'Kiss me.' He could hardly hear her broken

whisper over the soft sound of the waves, but he did hear the call her body made to his.

Gently he brushed his lips over hers. Then as passion fired through him he demanded more, pushing her back against the wet sand, heedless of the waves spilling over them as he covered her body with his.

Bianca couldn't believe she'd asked him so boldly to kiss her or that now she was lying in the soft surf of the Bahamas, practically naked with the man she thought she hated. She didn't hate him. She might hate herself for wanting him. She certainly hated him for awakening her passion, something she'd tried all her adult life to keep locked away. But she didn't hate *him*.

The water on her skin was exciting, but his touch, as he moved his hands over her, was almost unbearably erotic. With one hand under her shoulder, keeping his weight from her, his other hand skimmed over her thighs, her hips and up to her waist. All the time she was aware of his aroused state, pressing hard against her, demanding and tempting all at the same time.

She'd never done anything like this before. No man had ever touched her like this, and she trembled as he began to kiss down her neck, oblivious to the water rushing over them in a way that only heightened her senses, making every touch of his more powerful.

Her arms were wound around his neck, but as he kissed down her throat she spread her hands over his wet back, enjoying the strength that emanated from him. She'd never had a man so naked against her body, never felt the sizzle of skin against skin, but as he returned his kiss in a trail of blazing heat up to her lips, she had to stop herself gasping his name in pleasure.

As if he knew her torture, his tongue slipped between her lips and a sigh of pleasure finally escaped her as his hand cupped her breast, the sensation so new and heady she could hardly breathe. Was this what being loved by a man was like?

That thought sobered her mind. Liev didn't love her. He might desire her, but he didn't love her, and there was no way she was going to get carried away and give herself with such abandon to this man.

'No, stop.' She moved away from his kiss and pushed at his chest, trying to ignore the hardness beneath her palm. 'I can't do this.'

She scrambled to her feet, sand clinging to

her body as she trembled with unquenched desire and shock at what she'd wanted. She'd wanted to make love, right here on the beach in broad daylight with a man who was no better than Dominic. One was a gambler, the other a blackmailer, and both had used her for their own gain.

She watched as he, too, got to his feet and walked away from her, reaching down to collect their discarded garments. Was he seeking time for composure? She used those moments to press her wet hair against her head, smoothing down the disarray.

Then he turned to face her, his expression now the familiar mask of hardness, and regret pinched at her. 'I apologise.'

'It's just that…' She stopped short of spilling everything out. How did you tell the man you had just been kissing with such abandon that you were a virgin, that you had no experience of how to please him, how to enjoy the moment of intimacy she'd almost slipped into?

'Just what?' The words were snapped out and she knew he was angry, that he probably thought she'd led him on—and she had.

'I just need a bit of time.' She was stumbling over her words, the passion he'd ignited within her muddling her senses and making any kind of rational thought impossible. 'What I mean is, I hadn't expected that.'

'By *that*, I assume you mean the desire to kiss me, the need to feel my touch, or that you wanted me as much as I wanted you, regardless of everything else?'

She blushed and knew denial was useless. Instead she looked firmly at him. 'Yes, that is exactly what I mean.'

'We should get back. I expect you would like to change before dinner?'

She walked towards him and took the cover-up and her glasses from him, instinctively putting both on as a shield from his hungry gaze. As she walked beside him, the beauty of the island calmed her ruffled nerves and she wondered at what had just happened, but more alarming was the fact that she had wanted more.

Liev watched Bianca walk along the terrace after dinner; her shoulders were tense and all evening her conversation had been stilted. She was obviously not as comfortable with being here with him as he'd first thought. Especially after the kiss they'd shared at the water's edge. That had been so wildly passionate he'd hardly been able to drag himself off her when she'd demanded he stop. It had taken every last bit of his control to do that.

He walked out into the evening warmth and stood close behind her, and with her hair swept up, he longed to kiss her delicate neck, longed to resume what had been started just hours ago in the waves.

Gently he placed his hands on her shoulders and moved closer still, the urge to press his lips to her skin ever stronger. She didn't pull away and beneath his hands he could feel her shoulders rise and fall as her breathing deepened. He lowered his head and inhaled her scent, floral and intoxicatingly sexy.

Still she didn't pull away. Instead she leant back against him, tilting her head slightly to allow him access to the softness of her skin. As his lips met her skin, tasting her, she drew in a ragged breath and he knew she was far from indifferent to him. She wanted him as much as he wanted her.

'You feel it too.' He breathed the words against her skin, becoming more caught up in the desire he'd been keeping locked away since the auction, when she'd been so angry passion had blazed in her eyes. Now he wanted that anger to be nothing but passion.

She shook her head, the movement small

and indecisive. She was still battling with the desire which had sparked angrily to life between them the moment their paths had collided.

'No,' she whispered, but he knew that denial was the furthest thing from the truth that had ever passed those sweet lips of hers.

He trailed a finger down her neck and saw her quiver and arch away from him, and he knew that he was pushing her over the edge, just as he was himself. 'Why deny the inevitable?'

'Because I have to.'

'Why, when there is so much passion between us, so much desire? It is that very passion and desire that is keeping you here right now, when you could walk into the house and to your room. I wouldn't follow you there. I meant what I said earlier. Nothing will happen unless you want it to.'

He slid his hands down her arms and he stepped closer still, until there was barely a whisper of air between them. He wanted her so much, but he had to be patient, had to wait for the right time.

'Then you will accept that I can't do this, can't give in to whatever it is,' she murmured.

'But you admit it's there? You feel it, don't

you, Bianca?' He kissed a trail down her neck to her bare shoulders, breathing in the scent of her skin, tasting her and making staying in control all the harder for it.

Bianca closed her eyes and leant back against Liev's strong body. Heat seared through her as his lips kissed her neck again and she knew she should stop it, knew it wasn't what she needed, but it was so what she wanted.

'Yes, I feel it too.' The husky whisper which came from her was like no other sound she'd heard before. What was this power he had over her?

'I can't fight it much longer.' The words, whispered into her hair, sent a shiver of excitement down her spine, and she bit down on her bottom lip trying to hold on to herself.

His hands slid down her arms and she turned to look at him over her shoulder, but his lips brushed hers and she closed her eyes, no longer able to resist this new pleasure. A soft sigh escaped her as he kissed her so gently and persuasively, coaxing more from her with the skill of an accomplished lover.

His hand splayed across her cheek, keeping her head where he wanted it as he deepened the kiss. Driven by a force she had no control over, she turned as his arms wrapped around her, pressing her body against the hardness of his.

His lips left hers and she dragged in air, searching the slate grey of his eyes, looking for reassurance, but all she saw was hungry desire. Desire she had no experience of dealing with.

Just as she was about to pull away, to tell him it couldn't happen, he claimed her lips again in such a hard and demanding kiss she could no longer think. Heat which had been curling from a deep and secret place within her burst into flames, engulfing her so quickly she could hardly breathe.

She entwined her arms around his neck, pulling herself up against him, and the fire heated as she felt the evidence of his desire. This wasn't just part of the deal. He really wanted her. Euphoria took her higher as his tongue plundered her mouth, coaxing and demanding more from her. Again those ever-present doubts surfaced. She couldn't give more. Not to this man.

She pushed her hands against his chest and pulled back, breaking the kiss, but his arms held her firmly against him. She shook her head. 'We shouldn't be doing this, Liev.'

His eyes narrowed as he continued to hold

her against him. Beneath the palms of her hands she could feel the rapid rise and fall of his hard and muscular chest. That in itself was almost enough to tip her over the edge.

'Why not?' His fierce words jolted her back to her senses and she pushed against him once more, thankful when he let her go. Quickly she moved away from him, away from temptation.

'What we have isn't real.'

'Our engagement may not be, but this desire is. Are you so cold and hard you can ignore it and turn away from it that easily?' He stalked past her back into the living room and poured himself a drink. The sound of the liquid filling the glass was almost too loud.

He thought her cold? Well, so much the better. 'Yes, I am. We have a business arrangement and I am not in the habit of getting intimate with my clients.'

He took a big gulp and looked at her, icy coldness in his eyes. 'That's not how it seemed this afternoon, Bianca.'

She sighed softly. 'Whatever you might think of me, I'm not used to this sort of arrangement.'

'What sort is that? A lovers' weekend away?'

'It's not something I've done before.' If she told him she was inexperienced, would that dissuade him from looking for more than she could give?

'You have never slipped away for a weekend of passion with your lover?' The incredulity in his voice was clear.

'No.' She couldn't quite tell him she had never had a lover. Maybe now was a good time to say goodnight. The incredulity in his voice left her in no doubt that he was more than used to such weekends. She just wasn't ready for that yet. 'Goodnight, Liev.'

CHAPTER NINE

THE NEXT MORNING Bianca had woken to the sounds of the ocean and had blushed as she'd recalled how she'd behaved with such wanton abandon the previous afternoon, lying on the beach as waves had washed over them. What was more shocking and harder to deal with was the fact that she'd wanted Liev in a way that had been almost impossible to resist. Her whole body had been on fire with need. So much that she'd almost given in to him last night.

As the morning had passed they had made polite conversation and after a while Liev had gone for another swim, but this time she'd declined his offer. As she'd watched him go, the feeling that she was making a mistake, letting something special slip by, wouldn't leave her. She began to question why she'd stopped him last night, why she'd denied herself something every nerve in her body had demanded.

She didn't know that answer, didn't want to know it either. All she did know was if he ever kissed her again she wouldn't be able to stop. Every nerve in her body was on high alert, the simmering attraction she'd felt from the beginning now a desire-driven madness.

What was it about Liev? Could she really be in love with him? Had she found the same love Lucia had written about in her letter all those years ago? The words she'd read so many times came back to her, strangely fitting what she felt right now.

For is that not what love does? I would not change a moment of it, even though you are not entirely mine and I not entirely yours.

She was not Liev's fiancée. She had no right to feel anything for him, let alone this strange emotion that felt painfully like love. That thought was knife-like in her heart because, right now, cameras were being set up and her make-up was about to be done and she would be going out to face everyone as Liev's fiancée.

'Are you ready?' Liev joined her, his firm stance as he looked at her one that would not take no for an answer. At least once this was over and the visit to her grandfather done, they could finally go their separate ways. She was sure the shelter interview and this photoshoot would achieve much more than he'd originally demanded of the deal.

'Ready,' she lied, and she followed him out to the beach where the first shoot was planned. Posing so boldly for the camera was not something she was used to. She'd never invited the attentions of the press or magazines like this, which was probably why they'd instantly jumped at the chance.

The cameras clicked and Bianca posed, her body pressed close against Liev. Every move she made intensified the fire of awareness within her. All she could think about was that kiss yesterday, the one which had left her yearning for more, needing to know the joy of loving a man. Would that have happened if she hadn't stopped things last night?

'Have you set a date yet?' the interviewer asked as they took the final shot. 'And where will the wedding be? Here?'

Bianca blinked. She hadn't rehearsed any answers to their questions. Yesterday's moment of intimacy with Liev had completely thrown her off her usual organised course.

'Nothing is set yet.' Liev came to her rescue as he took her hand and lifted it to his lips. The camera she thought had been packed away clicked once more as she looked up at him. 'We are enjoying being together for now, are we not, Bianca?'

'That's it. That's the one.' The photographer's ecstatic voice hardly registered as she looked into Liev's eyes. The icy grey had softened as desire blended within them. Desire she knew was echoed in her eyes, but it was the intensity of them, the potent power of that seductive look, which almost made her knees buckle.

He lowered his head and kissed her—slowly, lingering so sensuously she closed her eyes and gave herself up to the moment. Then it ended. He pulled away and a chill swirled around her despite the warm wind and afternoon sun.

'Thank you,' Liev said as he turned to shake hands with the interviewer, but Bianca just wanted them gone, wanted back the peace that had surrounded the small villa as they'd arrived.

The sun was low in the sky, but Liev didn't feel the happiness he should feel as he stood and looked out over the ocean. The photoshoot had gone well. Bianca had been amazing, providing plenty of photos that could be used to show how much they were in love. She'd been so convincing he'd almost believed it too. But he'd been deceiving himself.

Try as he might, he couldn't fight the attraction he had for Bianca. She had unlocked the man he could have been if his life had taken a different course, the man who wanted love and happiness, just as his parents had enjoyed before everything went spectacularly wrong. But he wasn't that man any more and never could be again. One disastrous affair had seen to that.

'It's so peaceful here. You can almost forget the rest of the world exists,' Bianca whispered as she joined him on the balcony, the warm evening breeze moving through her dark hair as he turned to look down at her. This was a much softer version of the woman he'd outbid at the auction for a bracelet. During the time they'd been together as a couple he'd fallen harder and harder for her, until he knew he couldn't get enough of her.

What would she say if he told her he wanted to scoop her up and take her to the big bed he'd slept in alone last night and make her completely his? Would she welcome his touch, his kiss and his possession?

'Thank you.'

'For what?' His thoughts were muddled as heat infused him at the image of her in his bed.

'For bringing me here.' Her voice had a delicate wobble and he clenched his hands into fists to prevent himself reaching for her, pulling her into his arms and kissing away that worry. 'I know it's for the benefit of the exclusive, but thank you.'

'Is it true, that you have never spent time with a man like this, that you've never had a holiday romance?' He was still getting his head round the fact that a woman as sexy and alluring as Bianca had never gone away with a man.

She blushed and looked down. 'Yes.'

Now he couldn't help himself. He reached out and lifted her chin, forcing her to look at him. Apprehension showed in her eyes as well as that ever-increasing vulnerability. Had he pushed her too far in his pursuit of revenge? 'I'm sorry to have put you in this position. I never intended it to be this way.'

It had all been about keeping her from her latest trinket, but he suspected even that wasn't the truth. Whatever was going on with the bracelet, she'd stood up to him, fought her battles hard and kept her side of the deal.

The gentle breeze moved her hair across her

face as she looked up at him with an expression of innocence. Gently he pushed her hair back and tenderness squeezed at his chest. If only he wasn't the heartless man life had made him, he knew he could love her.

'I needed the bracelet,' she said softly, her eyes searching his, but no trace of anger in her voice.

'I know,' he whispered, guilt pressing down on him.

'You thought I was just being frivolous, buying myself jewellery?' Her words, though barely above a whisper, still held the injustice of that. 'It's not like that at all.'

'No, I don't think it is. There are many things about you that I have got wrong, Bianca.'

'Such as?'

'I believed you were a cold woman. One who knew exactly what she wanted and went for it, but I was wrong. The woman I see now is someone completely different. She is soft and loving, loyal and innocent, making me want things I can't have, things I don't deserve.'

'What things?' The cracked whisper sent a lust-filled heat racing around him.

'Affection.' He meant love, but that was a word he'd thought he'd never use out loud again. Bianca had done something to him, touched a part of his heart that had frozen the day he'd buried his father and sworn revenge and later had been shattered by a woman's betrayal.

'Everyone deserves affection.'

'I've done bad things, Bianca. I'm not the kind of man your grandfather would wish you to date, let alone become engaged to.'

'You've blackmailed me, deceived my grandfather and all of New York's society with our engagement and made me an accomplice in that deceit. What could be worse?'

If he told her of his past, about what had made him the man he was today, would it end this madness he was feeling? Would it stop the thoughts of making her truly his? Of course it would. A woman like Bianca Di Sione would want nothing to do with a criminal, even if his childhood record had been wiped away, as if those years in prison had never happened. But they had and he'd never forget them.

'I am what I am today, cold and calculating, because I had to learn to survive on my own, to fend for myself and fight my own battles—literally.' For a moment his mind raced back to those dark days on the streets of St Petersburg.

She reached up and touched his face, her

palm soft against his skin, and he bit down hard to prevent himself from pulling her against him. She was seriously testing him. He caught her hand in his, her eyes widening with shock as he held her wrist. Her gaze held his, a hint of the strength he'd first seen in her coming forward.

'I was in prison, Bianca—for five years.'

She gasped and the horrified look on her face told him all he needed to know. 'What for?' she asked, trepidation in those whispered words.

'For trying to stay alive.'

'I don't understand.'

No, she wouldn't. How could she when she'd never worried or wanted for anything? A protected princess.

'After my parents died, I had no choice but to live rough on the streets of St Petersburg. I stole to eat and fought for a safe place to sleep. One day I was caught stealing bread and potatoes for myself and the younger kids.' The embittered words snapped from him as he remembered the day he'd arrived at the prison, the hell of the place shaping who he now was.

'That was the home you mentioned the other day? How old were you—when you went to prison?'

'Thirteen.'

Why hadn't she backed away? Why hadn't she pulled herself free of him in disgust, knowing she could truthfully add *thief* to the charges she'd already laid on him? He let go of her and turned away, hardly able to bear the suspense of waiting for her to do just that. Why had he told her? He'd never let anyone know and had gone to great lengths to cover up that part of his past.

Bianca watched as Liev turned away from her. She should be glad. He was allowing her to walk away, but something held her there. This wasn't like that night ten years ago when she'd overheard the bets being made by the boy at school she'd fallen in love with. He'd been betting on whether she'd sleep with him by the end of the prom. She'd been used and the humiliation of that had given her a resilience she'd never known.

She'd been used again, but this time she knew the facts. All of them, from his sad childhood to the reason he was blackmailing her today. The two inextricably linked. She knew this and now as she watched Liev standing alone and proud on the edge of the beach, she felt her heart melt and fill with love for him, for the child he'd been and the man he'd become.

The past few days she'd wanted nothing more than for Liev to kiss her. Deep down, on a level she'd never experienced before, she also knew that if he did so again, it wouldn't stop there. There was no doubt in her mind that he was the man she'd been waiting for. They might not share a long-lasting love as she'd always dreamt it would be, but right now on this island they would be lovers.

'None of that matters, Liev.' She moved towards him and saw his shoulders stiffen and ached to touch him.

'How can you say that?' The gruffness of his voice told her he was struggling with his emotions as much as she was.

'Because nothing matters. Nothing at all. Your past or mine. Not even the future.' She reached out and touched her hand to his arm, felt the rigidness become more taut beneath her palm. 'All that matters is this moment right now.'

He turned towards her, stroked his hand against her hair. 'How can I have ever thought you were cold and emotionless?'

'Everyone hides something, but I can't hide from you any more. I want you to kiss me,

Liev.' A nervous flutter skittered in her stomach as she said the words. Would he want to kiss her if he knew how inexperienced she was? She'd never even kissed a man before him, not really kissed. That tantalising taste of what could be had left her wanting more.

'Are you sure?' His eyes darkened as his fingers tangled in her hair, bringing her closer to him.

She'd never been so sure of anything in her life. 'I've been hiding for too long and tonight I want to change that.'

His eyes, dark and swirling with desire, searched hers, and then, so slowly the anticipation was almost unbearable, he lowered his head and kissed her, gently at first, but as she wrapped her arms around his neck, it became harder and more demanding. His fingers clutched her hair, holding her just where he needed her, and the flames of passion he'd been stirring since the moment they first met exploded into life.

'You have no idea what you do to me, Bianca.' He broke the kiss and looked at her, his fingers stroking her cheek, the tenderness of the touch almost unbearable. She felt his breathing, deep and uneven, as his chest rose and fell against her, sparking more desire.

Did he have any idea what he was doing to her? Did he know she wanted to cast aside her ten-year vow and allow herself to love a man, in every sense of the word—even if it was just for one night? She was under no illusions it would be more, but maybe, just maybe, love could change that.

'Neither do I,' she said, and a soft blush crept over her cheeks, but she had to tell him this was new to her. 'I have never done this, Liev.'

He frowned. 'Seduce a man?'

Was she seducing him? She had no idea how to. Embarrassment flooded her and she lowered her gaze. 'Seduction is not something I'm well practised in.'

His hands moved to hold her arms and he held her gently away from him and looked at her, his expression hard and serious. 'Is that so?'

Her heart was thumping hard as she waited for the rejection that would surely follow such a revelation. Inside she was eighteen again. Uncertainty filled her, almost dousing the flames of desire which were leaping inside her. The only difference was that this time she didn't want to walk away, didn't want to deny herself the chance of loving.

Slowly she nodded, too afraid her voice

would fail her if she tried to say anything. Nervously she bit her lower lip and looked up at him, his hard expression almost unreadable. If he was going to push her away, she wished he'd just do it, instead of prolonging the agony.

His hands slid down her arms. Then he took her hand in his. Without saying anything, he led her from the garden, through the homely comfort of the living room to his bedroom. With every step her heart thumped in nervous anticipation. Never had she imagined the moment she would give herself completely to a man to be like this.

'Liev,' she whispered as he closed the door of his bedroom. The sound of the ocean lapping the sands was all she could hear other than her pounding heart.

'Don't say anything, Bianca.' His voice almost broke with huskiness as he pulled her into his arms. 'Just feel.'

She closed her eyes as his lips claimed hers, coaxing the flames of passion to rise once more. His hands skimmed down her sides to hold her hips, pulling her against him, proving he wanted her. She sighed into his mouth, revelling in the strength of his body. She didn't want him to stop now. She was his— and maybe she had always been.

When he let go of her and stepped back, she swayed like a newly bloomed flower in the wind. She was light-headed and the throbbing heat his kiss had evoked was almost too much pleasure. All she wanted was to close her eyes again.

'I feel as if my whole life has been waiting for this moment.' His words were still husky and heavily accented. 'And it will be special for you, I promise.'

She drew in a ragged breath as he looked at her, sizzling intent in his eyes. She wanted it to be special—for both of them. A time out of reality that could never be repeated. She wanted him, because he was the right man, the man she'd been waiting for, and alarming as it would be when she left the island and returned to her real life, he was the man she loved.

She took a deep breath, one born out of anticipation, and moved against him and placed her palms on his chest, feeling the strength beneath them. Slowly she raised herself on the tips of her toes and brushed her lips against his. If she had to feel the moment, so did he. As he responded, her fingers opened his shirt, with an ease which astounded her. She dropped back down off her toes and trailed her fingers through the dark hair which covered his chest, marvelling at its silky smoothness—and her boldness.

She pressed her lips against his skin, inhaling the intoxicating scent of the man she'd fallen in love with, committing it to memory. He lifted her chin, forcing her to look up at him.

'Is this really what you want?' Harshness had crept back into his words and his expression was stern, as if he was fighting for control.

'Yes.' She could hardly speak as her pulse seemed to be jumping in her throat. 'But if you don't…'

She didn't manage to finish her sentence before he claimed her mouth in a hard and hungry kiss which took her breath completely away. She gave in to the desire which was throbbing within her, urging her on, and kissed him back as if her life depended on it. Maybe it did.

He moved against her, propelling her backwards towards the bed, each step becoming more urgent. He didn't stop kissing her as they fell onto the bed, the soft white covers wrapping around them as their bodies entwined.

This was wild and so much more intense than she'd ever imagined. If this was how he kissed, really kissed, she didn't think she'd survive being made love to. His lips, bruising and demanding, stoked the flames higher as his hands roamed over her body, the flimsy sundress little protection against the heat of his touch.

Her hands began exploring him, spreading over his back, relishing the strength and then moving under his open shirt and over his skin. She'd never touched a man this way, never been caressed like this, and didn't want it to stop.

His fingers teased her hardened nipples and she gasped with the shock of pleasure which raced through her. He began to kiss her throat, moving lower and lower, and she lay there, eyes closed, enjoying the sensation of fire each kiss left behind. His fingers began to unfasten the small buttons on the front of her blue dress, but the same impatience she felt made him pull hard at the fabric until the buttons yielded and the dress tore.

She should have been horrified, but she didn't care about that; all she wanted was to feel his touch on her breasts, his skin against hers. In response, she pushed his shirt from his shoulders, forcing him to briefly release her as he levered himself up, and virtually tore the shirt from him.

He paused and looked at her, his chest rising and falling rapidly with each desire-driven breath. 'You are more beautiful than I could ever have imagined.' Then with a wicked smile he removed his jeans, until he stood before her in black briefs which did little to conceal his hardened state of arousal.

She sat up and began to undo the remainder of her buttons. He placed one hand on the bed and leant towards her, the muscles in his arm firming as he did so, snagging her attention. 'No more,' he said gruffly. 'That is for me to do, but first I need to take care of a practical issue.'

'Practical?' Her mind stumbled. What was he talking about?

'The small issue of contraception.'

How had she forgotten that? What kind of idiot would he think she was? She watched him closely for any hint of shock at her brazen behaviour, but was more shocked when he opened his bedside drawer, took out his wallet and produced the necessary foil packet. Did he always keep his island home so prepared?

Before she had a chance to dwell on that, he'd wrapped his hands around her ankles, then slipped off her sandals, his grey eyes watching her intently. She blushed as his attention lowered, to her exposed breasts, and had to force herself to stay there beneath his scrutiny instead of giving in to the innocent urge for modesty.

He stroked his fingers up her legs, over her knees and under her dress and she was transfixed by the fire of need which raged in her. Just when she thought he was going to touch her intimately, he moved back, leaving her aching. But that ache was soon quenched as he moved over her, lowering his body onto hers as he claimed her lips in a kiss so wild and demanding she gasped aloud.

As if driven by her response, he slid his legs between hers and she could feel the heat and hardness of him. All she could think about was moving against him, finding a way, any way, to get closer, and she became irritated by her half-undressed state. She could feel his bare chest against her naked breasts, but it wasn't enough. Nowhere near enough.

His hands moved down between their bodies as he lifted his weight from her and in seconds the remainder of the buttons were undone and her dress pushed away from her. Underwear was now the only barrier between them.

Giving in to an instinct that was new and exciting, she lifted one leg and with pointed toes trailed it up his leg. The growl of pleasure he gave emboldened her further and she moved her palms against his buttocks, pressing him against her until a string of muttered Russian words flew from his lips.

'If you continue with this, I am not going to remember your inexperience and will lose all control.' He looked down at her, his arms braced as he held his upper body above her, but still his erection pressed against her.

She smiled at him, liking the power over him she now had. 'In that case.' The taunt in her voice was clear as she wrapped her other leg around him, forcing him so close that if it wasn't for their underwear she would be his.

The thought sent heat spiralling through her. She wanted this man to claim her, to take her most precious gift, because somehow she'd fallen in love with him. She had no idea when, but in their constant battles for control, she'd lost her heart to him. She was already his; no matter what happened now, she was his.

'Bianca, have mercy on me.' Surprised at the hoarseness of his voice, Liev claimed her lips once more in a kiss so mind-blowing he very nearly lost control right there and then. What was it about this woman that was so different from any other?

'Never,' she gasped as he pulled away from her and looked down at her, hair spread across the pillow and eyes closed in total abandon.

He moved down, trailing his fingers over her stomach until he reached the final physical barrier between them, and as he slid off the bed, he pulled her panties down those delicious legs that had caught his attention the first time he'd seen her. Now that demure and controlled woman was his, her passion so fierce it almost burned him.

She opened her eyes and looked at him, a nervous question in them. She was so beautiful it broke his heart. Did he have one to break? He'd always thought that it had been replaced by stone the day his life had changed.

He grabbed the foil packet he'd pulled out of his wallet earlier, removed his underwear and, with her eyes hungrily devouring him, rolled on the condom. He'd intended to take it slowly, to try to be mindful of her claim of inexperience, but as he covered her body with his, hers welcomed his so expertly he lost that final thread of control and thrust into her, deep and hard.

Her fingernails dug into his shoulders, and with her head pushed back deep into the pillow, she cried out in shock and pleasure. He stilled, the effort making his body shake. She was more than inexperienced. She was a virgin.

'Don't stop, Liev, please.'

She moved her hips, urging him to continue, and that final thread of control he'd been hanging on to snapped. He moved inside her, and as she wrapped her legs around him again, keeping him deep inside her, he was lost. Waves of pleasure, so big he thought he might drown, cascaded over him, and he knew this moment would change things. It would change him, change everything he'd been driven to do since he was a young boy.

She gasped his name as her release swept her away, dragging him with her until he lay over her, shaking in a way he'd never done before. All he could think about was that he'd taken her virginity, stolen it with his deceit and lies, because there was no way she would have surrendered such a precious gift if she'd known all he wanted was revenge on ICE, revenge that would destroy her brother too.

With his breathing still ragged and his body still humming, he moved off her, disgusted with himself. He'd taken a woman's innocence in the name of revenge. What kind of man did that make him?

'Liev?' He heard her startled question as he

strode to the bathroom, but he couldn't look at her, not yet. She would see the anger and disgust blazing in his eyes and she didn't deserve that. She didn't deserve any of this.

Bianca heard the shower and lay there, unable to move. She wanted to run back to her room and hide from the anger she'd seen blazing in his eyes and the contempt as he'd glanced back at her.

Should she have told him, made it clear that she was totally inexperienced—a virgin?

What had she done to change things so drastically? The passion had been so intense her body had burned for his; now it was icy cold with shock and she realised she was shivering. Whatever was wrong, she wasn't going to run and hide. Bianca Di Sione didn't hide; she faced things head-on. Always had done and always would do.

She pulled the delicate and creased fabric of her dress together, buttoning it up and wishing her hands would stop shaking. When he came out of that bathroom, she was standing in front of the mirror brushing down her hair, smoothing away the just-tumbled-in-bed look.

Their eyes met in the mirror and she blinked at the image of him naked but for a skimpy white towel around his hips. The passion she'd just experienced flared to life again and she wondered if this was to be the moment they would go back to bed—if they were lovers.

'You should have told me, Bianca.' He looked at her in the mirror, those icy grey eyes full of regret. 'You should have made it clear you were not just inexperienced. You should have said you were a virgin.'

Indignation rose, as did the need to protect herself, just as she'd done ten years ago. 'And if I had?'

He walked over to her and stood before her, hardly caring about his state of undress. She looked up at him, trying to ignore the increasingly rushing pulse just from being so close to him.

'You were a virgin and I am not your fiancé. Hell, I'm not even your lover.' The softened features of his face she'd kissed just moments ago were now hard and set in fierce lines.

'No, you are my blackmailer. You're no better than Dominic. He'd placed bets with his friends at the school prom he'd take my virginity. Thankfully I'd found out, played him at his own game. But you stooped even lower.'

'I would not have done that if I'd known.' The anger in his voice was so clear it cut at her delicate heart, crushing it cruelly. 'I made a mistake.'

She gasped. 'Don't say that.' Why was he pushing her away?

'It shouldn't have happened, Bianca.'

'Where does that leave us now, Liev? What happens now?'

He stalked across the room to stare out at the gardens bathed in light from the setting sun. 'We leave tomorrow morning as planned.'

She wanted to go to him, to ask what she'd done, but her pride and ever-present need for survival kept her from doing that. Instead she stood with as much decorum as her crumpled dress would allow and lifted her chin in the defiant gesture she always did when life hurt.

'We still have to visit my grandfather. That was part of the deal.'

'Very well. You kept your side of the deal today at the photoshoot. I will honour that.'

CHAPTER TEN

As he approached Bianca's family home, Liev looked at the large white house set in immaculately maintained grounds and had to suppress his anger. This was what his mother could have enjoyed if ICE hadn't duped his father so cruelly. Instead his mother had died in poverty and pain, broken-hearted after watching the man she loved drink himself into oblivion, believing he was nothing but a failure.

He tried to refocus his thoughts, bring them back to the present. Bianca had been stoically silent during the flight back from his island retreat. Now, as he stopped his car outside the imposing front doors, he glanced across at her. She looked much younger and more vulnerable than she'd ever done before. It was more than just the light make-up she wore today or the soft floating sundress, which caressed her body, reminding him how he'd done the same.

Every emotion she was feeling was exposed. A sensation he, too, felt and he didn't like it one bit. She'd changed him, made him think differently, feel differently, and he couldn't allow sentiment to get in the way of his plans—not now—not ever.

'Grandfather will be resting for the remainder of the day,' she said as she got out of the car and walked towards the sweeping front veranda of the house. Discreet members of staff came out to take his car to be parked. This was most definitely high-society living.

'I trust he is well enough to meet with us later, even if only for a short while?'

'Of course. That is the main reason we are here. He plans to join us before dinner this evening.'

The thought of being vetted by her grandfather sat uncomfortably with him. Naturally the old man would want his granddaughter to be happy, but what would he say if he knew she was being blackmailed? For a bracelet? What would the old man think of him if he knew he'd taken her innocence—her virginity—as part of that blackmail?

He watched as Bianca greeted the staff with genuine affection and didn't miss the way they responded with fondness. The sound of her light laughter caught him unawares as she laughed at something the maid had said. Before he had any other opportunity to say anything, she turned and smiled at him, the laughter of moments ago still in her eyes.

'This way.'

He walked with her up the wide staircase, the intimacy of being in her family home not lost on him. How many other men had she brought home to meet her grandfather? From the comfortable way she was dealing with this, it was something she was used to doing.

What he hadn't expected was to be shown into a suite so large his own childhood home would have fitted into it twice over. She closed the door and blushed, not able to meet his questioning gaze.

'This is the principle guest suite and where we can change for dinner, or rest until we head back to New York this evening.'

Liev bit back against the urge to walk out right now and go back to New York. How could he have thought coming here was a good idea? He could feel his frozen emotions thawing, more rapidly than he was comfortable with, and knew the iron-strong will which served as his barrier against everyone was failing. He shouldn't feel anything for Bianca. She was a means to an end, a tool which turned the wheel of his revenge.

He could understand her need to pacify her grandfather about the engagement. It was making headlines, and even if he was frail and elderly, the old man would want to know who it was his granddaughter had become engaged to. But being here, in the home he'd raised all the Di Sione children, including Dario, was too intimate, too personal.

Just as sleeping with Bianca had been. Not only sleeping with her, but taking her virginity, damn it. Guilt continued to eat away at him over that.

'I have no intention of staying here any longer than necessary.' He snapped the words out as he looked at the view from the doors which opened out onto a magnificent balcony. 'It's not as if the engagement is permanent. I only agreed to this so you could do what was needed to put your grandfather's mind at rest. Nothing more.'

He didn't need to look at Bianca to know she was bristling with indignation. He could feel it in the hot afternoon air.

'I apologise for the inconvenience, but just because you are ruthless and cold-hearted doesn't mean I am. I care about my grandfather, and even if this damn engagement is fake, I will not give him cause to worry about me. I played along with your photoshoot, gave you all you needed and more, so now you will afford me the same courtesy.'

He turned to look at her, hostility rushing off her in waves as she made yet more demands on him. The vulnerable woman he'd begun to glimpse on their last dates, the one who'd tantalisingly revealed herself over the past few days, had now gone. And why wouldn't she? This was her family home, her territory. Just as she'd been emotionally exposed at his island villa, so he was here.

'I will do my best to convince your grandfather I am worthy of calling myself your fiancé.' Why it mattered to him when all he wanted was to avenge his parents was beyond reason right now, adding to those exposed emotions he was desperate to hide.

'Thank you. Now if you will excuse me, I must just go and see my grandfather quickly.'

Bianca rushed from the room, desperate to calm herself before she saw her grandfather, but with the hum of desire still heating her body and the anger at herself for having responded to Liev's expert touch, she doubted the short walk to her grandfather's suite would do that. The hours on the plane, then trapped with Liev in his car, had been too much. The memory of her night in his bed was burning in her mind, so much she doubted it would ever fade.

Unnerved by how she'd all but begged him to make love to her, she smoothed down her dress and took a deep breath before knocking on her grandfather's door. His frail voice called her in and her insides contracted, sure he would want to know if she had made any progress with the bracelet.

'Hi,' she said as she walked in, trying not to show how shocked she was by his ever-weakening health. Damn Liev and his blackmail. That emotion mixed uncomfortably with the passion she and Liev had shared and guilt added to the potent cocktail.

'Bianca,' he said with a smile, and he gestured for her to come closer. He took her hands in his and looked at the large diamond ring on her finger. 'It is true, then. My Bianca has finally succumbed to love.'

'Don't.' She smiled down at him, knowing he was only teasing. It was just a little too close to the truth. How had she even fallen for a man who used such underhand tactics as blackmail?

'I just want you to be happy, Bianca, and whatever you do, don't waste a chance of love if it comes along.' His words, though frail, were steeped in deeper meaning.

'No, I won't.' She had to paste a smile on her lips as she looked down at him. 'But you rest now and later you can meet Liev.'

As she walked back to the suite, the guilt of deceiving her grandfather weighed heavily on her mind. What would he say when the engagement ended? He would be heartbroken for her; she knew that much. What would anyone say when it became public knowledge? Would all the effort she'd put into Liev's acceptance by society be wasted as soon as word got out they were no longer engaged?

She could hear Liev talking on the phone as she opened the door to the suite. The Russian words were so alien to her that she had to stop and listen, but the coldness of his tone could not be mistaken. Whoever was on the other end of the phone had definitely angered him.

He met her gaze and ended the call. 'My assistant in St Petersburg.'

'Not bad news, I hope.'

'No, not all.' He stood and looked at her for a moment, as if seeing her for the first time. 'How was your grandfather?'

The fact that he'd asked knocked her emotionally off balance and she blinked back the urge to give in to the tears which had prickled in her eyes since she'd left the old man's rooms. She wished there was another way to get the bracelet. Not only was she lying to her grandfather and entire family, but she'd lost her heart and her virginity, given them away to a ruthless blackmailer who wasn't even capable of love.

'Frail, but looking forward to meeting you.'

'Are any of your brothers or sisters here too?' he asked as he sat down on the elegant white sofa, looking so relaxed it could almost be his home.

'No. It's just us here this evening.' She thought of Allegra and wished she was here to guide her, though not with dealing with Liev and his blackmail tactics. That she could manage herself. What she needed help with was the way he made her feel, the way her heart leapt and her pulse raced just from thinking about him. The way she missed him when he wasn't around. The way he'd awakened the woman within. It was all too real.

'You look tired,' he said as he stood up and came to her, guiding her to the sofa he'd just been sitting on. The genuine concern in his voice almost finished her. 'Sit down and relax.'

She sat down, a little surprised when he sat next to her, his knee touching hers as he moved closer. 'I know you don't have brothers or sisters, but do you have cousins or other family?' His mention of her family made her realise they still knew very little of each other. It shocked her to realise she wanted to know more about him, more about his family, his home.

'No, I was an only child, which was hard when my parents died.' He looked at her and she saw sadness in his eyes, the same sadness she felt when she thought of her parents. For him it was different. Not worse, just different. She could barely remember hers; he would have formed many memories with his.

Suddenly the need to talk washed over her like an incoming tide. 'I can hardly remember my mother and the only images I have of my father are from photos. I did have brothers and sisters though. You had nobody. That must have been hard.'

Liev watched her beautiful face. She looked so defenceless his heart constricted with pain, for her loss as well as his. She had weaved a spell on him, bringing him physically nearer to his goal, but emotionally further from it. Right at this moment, as he looked into the blue depths of her eyes, he wasn't sure if he still wanted the revenge on ICE he'd planned for so many years.

No. He pushed that thought away. Revenge was the only option, the only way to put right the past.

'I had nobody and that had unsavoury consequences at the time, but it made me the man I am today. It made me stronger.' He couldn't help but compare the time he'd spent on the streets of St Petersburg with her life here, growing up like a cosseted princess. Just being in this house dragged them further apart.

'It's strange how an event can shape your whole life,' she said earnestly, obviously thinking back to some hardship she had had to endure. Then he remembered what she'd said about her prom night. It had obviously affected her badly. He recalled how she'd ranked him as bad as that man. But he knew he was worse.

'At least you had a home and your grandfather.' He tried to keep the bitterness from his voice and his mind on the present. While she'd been living in luxury he'd been living through the hell of the regimented life of prison and all because his father had fallen victim to ICE, the company her brother now headed. Getting close to Dario would enable him to seek out those responsible for his father's downfall. 'And your brothers and sisters.'

She smiled at a secret memory and he felt strangely excluded. 'The twins were so naughty, although I think Dario has settled down now.'

Exactly the topic he wanted. 'The owner of ICE?'

'Yes.' She looked at him, surprise in her face briefly. 'But then being in the same market, you know all about him, I'm sure.'

'Not all.' He laughed softly, anything to keep the anger from boiling over. 'We are not competitors for business. Our products could complement each other's.'

'You should talk to him.'

'Oh, I intend to, but now may not be a good time. Isn't he about to launch his latest product? Maybe we shouldn't be talking about it. There is, after all, client confidentiality.'

She smiled at him, her guard dropped by happy memories being in her home had evoked. 'It seems you know anyway. It's what I've been working on for the past two weeks, and with just two more weeks to go, it's going to be a busy time. Just as well this interview should get you what you want. Then I can concentrate on that instead of playing the role of your fiancée.'

The barb hit home but he took it knowing he was finally getting to what he really needed to know.

'He took over the company and made it into a bigger success, I believe. Highly commendable.' Except for his ethics in pushing the company's past dealings under the table without any compassion for those who'd lost and suffered due to being all but robbed by ICE. His parents weren't the only ones. Finally he would get past Dario and confront those responsible.

'I should arrange a meeting for you with him.'

This was too easy. She was telling him all he needed to know in order to finally achieve his goals, even offering to arrange a meeting with Dario. 'I'd appreciate that.'

She stood up and looked down at him, and again he marvelled how the layers of her defences seemed to be coming away, almost before his eyes. How long would it be before he saw the real Bianca again?

He watched as she walked away to her room. He'd wanted to call her back, to pull her into his arms and tell her she didn't have to be alone tonight when they finally returned to New York, that he would keep her safe, but he stopped himself just in time. She'd never be safe from him.

Just one more charade to get through and that would be the hardest one. She had to convince her grandfather that what she and Liev were doing was real, that they did love one another. Under no circumstances did she want him worrying about her when he was so ill.

'This will mean a lot to my grandfather,' she said quickly, her mask of indifference returning, even if only briefly. With her hand still in Liev's, she made her way to the large lounge the family always entertained guests in.

'I don't want my grandfather tired. He is not well. All I want is to make his last days as happy and worry free as possible.'

She felt Liev glance at her as they walked but she didn't dare look at him. If she did and saw sympathy in his eyes, she might dissolve into a heap of tears right here.

'I will do my best not to upset him, although meeting your granddaughter's fiancé can't be easy.'

Bianca tried to remain calm and composed.

She didn't want her grandfather to see even a tiny hint that things weren't right. He never said much, but he always noticed everything. She could see him sitting in his favourite chair, watching them. Did they create a picture of happiness? From the look on his face, she thought they might be achieving that at least.

Liev greeted her grandfather with a firm handshake, regardless of the fact that he wasn't able to stand up and greet him properly. They sat together and she was aware of her grandfather's scrutiny as they made polite conversation about the weather and the house.

'You must make Bianca very happy.' She blushed as he launched into the protective parent mode, straight to the point as always.

'I hope so.' Liev's hand tightened around hers as he answered.

'She has never brought a man home before. I'm not even aware that she has dated before.'

'Grandfather,' Bianca scolded him. Liev didn't need to know such details, especially now, after he'd rejected her because of that innocence.

'I'm just doing my job, Bianca.' His words were as firm as an elderly man's could be, but there was humour in his eyes. Whatever the test was, Liev had passed it.

She stood up, knowing they were tiring him. 'We'll leave you to rest now.'

He had nodded at her, obviously more exhausted than he was letting her know. Liev took her hand and they walked towards the double doors of the lounge.

'Bianca.'

She turned as he called her name, her heart filling with love for the man who had raised her and protected her as best he could—and still was, if the past half an hour was anything to go by.

'Any news on the bracelet?'

Inwardly she deflated. That was the worst thing he could have asked. Why hadn't he done that when she'd gone to see him? Beside her she felt Liev stiffen and his fingers tightened on her hand.

'Not yet, but I'm hopeful that it won't be long.'

Liev felt Bianca become rigid at his side, felt her hand loosen its grip in his as if she wanted to escape, but he held hers tighter, keeping her right where he wanted her, right where he could find out exactly what was going on.

I'm hopeful that it won't be long. Those had been her exact words.

He forced down the bile which rose in his throat. He'd wrung himself out with guilt at taking her virginity, felt lower than he'd ever felt in his life for using her so appallingly when she'd talked of her growing affection, telling him that their pasts meant nothing. Then she'd told him of her prom night, adding to that guilt. All that must have been part of her game plan.

She'd been desperate to get her hands on the bracelet, to give it to her grandfather. She'd bartered something as precious as her virginity. Would she now throw herself at him again, as their time together drew to a close, just to ensure she got the piece?

Disgust rushed over him, hotly followed by annoyance. He'd believed her declarations of growing affection, believed that maybe, if it wasn't for his need to wipe out ICE, they could be lovers. She knew more about him now than many of his friends did. But obviously, he didn't know enough about her.

'We should change for dinner.' Her voice was light, but he heard the guilt lacing through it.

He wanted to tell her dinner wasn't a good idea and that he would be going straight back to his apartment in New York. But that first reaction gave way to a gut instinct which urged caution. If she could use him so shamelessly, he shouldn't have any remorse or guilt about finding out about Dario's new product—or using that information. He knew it was a phone, one that would revolutionise the market, but he had to know much more. Leaking half the story and expecting the share prices to fall enough for him to make a takeover was business suicide.

Despite what he thought of Bianca right now and the way she'd sold herself to him, he had to keep that connection going between them and, above all, put aside anything he'd begun to feel for her and remember his promise as he'd stood at his parents' graveside over twenty years ago.

'Maybe we can sort out our differences over dinner?' He lowered his voice, keeping it smooth, effectively offering an olive branch to her.

She stopped and looked up at him, hope lingering in her eyes. 'Yes, perhaps we can.'

He nodded in approval. 'Are we still changing for dinner?'

'I think it would be best. Grandfather would approve—if he does join us, that is.' There was a hint of anxiety in her voice and he suppressed the urge to offer comfort.

After he'd changed for dinner, he sat on the balcony, watching the sun set over an estate that made him seethe with anger for what his parents could have had if ICE hadn't been so mercenary. Dario Di Sione had pointedly ignored the fact that the company he now owned was only so lucrative because of the businesses it had wiped out. Liev's father had built his up from nothing, creating an inheritance for his only son, but had been duped by the cunning and underhand deal offered by ICE. Driven by the need to put the past right, Liev had rebuilt it from nothing using his knowledge, intuition and, above all, the need to survive, making it bigger and better. His father would be proud.

'Ready?' Bianca asked, dragging him back from the darkness of his black thoughts.

She looked beautiful, even more vulnerable and innocent if that was possible. How could he have fallen for her soft words, her assurances that all that mattered had been that night in his villa?

'You look lovely.' He spoke the truth but hoped to pick up the gauntlet where she'd thrown it and lull her into a false sense of security with loving words and gestures. This time he would be well and truly in charge.

'I don't think Grandfather will be joining

us, so I hope you don't mind standing on ceremony just to have dinner with me.'

'It will be a pleasure to dine one last time with my fiancée.'

'Last time?' She frowned, looking far more worried than she probably was. 'So you are happy that we have achieved all that was needed?'

'Yes. I strongly suspect that the exclusive on the island will more than clinch that deal.' He kept his voice free of the emotion raging through him. Everything was becoming too mixed up, getting too close to something real, exposing too many vulnerabilities, and he didn't like it one bit.

'And the bracelet?'

Did she now regret using her virginity to secure the bracelet? He smiled, fighting hard against the urge to tell her to forget the damn bracelet, but somehow he managed to hold it all together. 'I will have the bracelet delivered as soon as I am convinced the acceptance I wanted has been achieved.'

'Thank goodness,' she said as they left their suite and entered the large family dining room, the table looking odd set only for two. 'I'm going to be so busy with Dario's launch I won't have time to parade our engagement.'

He pulled out her chair and the temptation to place his hands on her shoulders, to kiss the back of her neck, almost made him miss the inadvertent opening she'd just presented.

Bianca closed her eyes and held her breath as Liev lingered briefly behind her chair. She could almost feel his hands on her shoulders and his lips against her skin. Her heart rate accelerated wildly and memories of just how good his kisses were heated her body.

What had they been talking about? The phone and its launch, yes. 'It is set to take over the market. There's nothing else out there that can do as much from just one handset. Business will be revolutionised with it.'

As she spoke, he walked around the table to take his place opposite her, and as he came into her line of vision, she remembered who she was talking to. He might be the man she'd fallen in love with, but he was also her brother's competitor.

'You must be very proud of your brother.' His dark eyes fixed her to the spot, sending a sizzle of desire spiralling through her. How could she still be feeling such attraction to him, when it was obvious that once they arrived back in New York their engagement would be over?

'I am, yes. He's worked hard and deserves this success.'

Liev raised his glass to her. 'To success—for all of us.'

She had the strangest sensation that there was another meaning hidden deep in that innocent toast and had been about to ask him what he meant when the housekeeper, Alma, discreetly entered the dining room with a message from her grandfather's nurse.

'Is Grandfather all right?' Bianca asked, alarmed.

'He is, but has asked to be excused this evening. He's very tired.'

'Of course. That's fine. I will slip in and say goodbye before I leave.' She lowered her gaze to the table, worried about her grandfather. He was getting frailer each time she saw him and his disappointment at not yet having the bracelet had been painfully clear. He must have thought her visit was not primarily to introduce Liev, but to reunite him with one of his much-talked-of Lost Mistresses. Sadly, she hadn't yet achieved that. She vowed that next time she visited would be different.

She turned her attention back to Liev. 'Would you mind if we left as soon as possible?'

She wanted to see her grandfather before it

got too late, reassure him that next time she came home she would have with her the bracelet. And she would. Whatever she had to do, she would have it for him.

CHAPTER ELEVEN

BIANCA HAD NEVER been more pleased to see
the weekend. Although it was Saturday, she'd
still had to work. All week she'd forced herself to concentrate on Dario's launch, now
just one week away, and not think at all about
the man she'd fallen in love with. She tried to
put aside her grandfather's words of advice
as she'd slipped into his dimly lit room to say
goodbye. What he'd seen between her and Liev
was just what he had needed to see and very
different from the reality. But he must have
sensed something because he'd warned her
about denying herself love.

With a frustrated sigh, she dragged her mind
back to the present and as far away from Liev
Dragunov as possible. She was just a week
away from the launch and should be focused
and alert, but she wasn't. If it wasn't the worry
of her grandfather and still not being able to

give him the bracelet filling her mind, it was that one night with Liev, in his arms as if nothing else had mattered, that haunted her. He took over her mind during the day and infused her dreams at night.

That one night was such a contrast to what had happened since they'd returned from the photoshoot exclusive. He'd dropped her off at her apartment after honouring his word of visiting her family home and meeting her grandfather as planned. The car journey from her Long Island family home had been tense, and each time she'd looked at him, he'd been stern, anger in every move he made, every word he'd said. He'd coolly bid her goodbye, as if they hadn't shared even a kiss before, and as the week had progressed, his silence had lengthened and she'd begun to wonder what had gone so wrong. And worse—if she would ever get the bracelet.

He hadn't even contacted her when their engagement exclusive hit the news stands. That photo of him about to kiss her as she'd looked adoringly into his eyes was just about everywhere she went. She thought the saying was that the camera never lied, but it did. They looked so in love, so blissfully happy in that photo, but the reality was so far removed from that loving image it made her feel sick.

She paced her apartment, replaying every word, every touch, and each time the humiliation increased. What kind of fool was she? No longer able to stay inside, she grabbed her purse and left. A walk in the sunshine would help, as would being among the families and couples who would be enjoying Central Park on a sunny Saturday afternoon. When she came back she would be more composed and would send Liev an email request for the bracelet. She didn't think she could talk to him on the phone and much less face-to-face.

As the elevator doors swished open, her heart thudded to an abrupt stop, her breath caught in her throat, and all she could do was stand and stare. Standing there in all his magnificence was the man she'd unwittingly given her heart to. How should she greet him? What should she say to the man who'd woken the woman within her, then virtually abandoned her?

'We need to talk.' His tone was stern, his expression hard, and a lump of dread filled her throat.

'Is the feature not to your liking?' She hurled her tart words at him as she moved past him and into the lobby, vaguely aware of the doorman's curious glance, the first person to witness discord between New York's latest celebrity lovers. That discord would pave the way for their eventual separation.

Before he could reply, she pushed open the door and walked onto the bustle of the street, hailing a taxi. If he wanted to talk to her, he'd just have to come with her. As if he'd read her mind, he was beside her in the taxi before she could say anything. She glared at him, not sure whether to be angry or pleased he'd followed her.

'Central Park. Seventy-second Street.' She had no intention of asking Liev where he'd like to go. She was going to do what she'd planned—a walk to Bethesda Fountain, where she could find some shade to relax in and try to stop thinking about last weekend, the way it had changed her life and how nothing could ever be the same again. At least that had been her original plan.

The taxi moved through the afternoon traffic and the silence stretched between her and Liev, as it had done all week, but she wasn't going to be the one to break it. She wasn't going to be needy and ask him why he hadn't called her. She was only his fake fiancée, after all. What rights did she have? *If you were his fake fiancée, you should never have gone to bed with him.* The mocking voice in her mind intensified as her anger increased. She'd been such a fool. It was worse than her prom night because she'd wanted it to happen, wanted to be his, even for one night. She'd been swept away by the passion of being whisked off from everyday life to an idyllic island setting. Had that been his intention all along?

As soon as the taxi pulled over, Liev got out, settling the fare before she had a chance. She stepped out into the sunshine; her earlier bravado, brought on by the shock of seeing him standing there when the elevator doors opened, vanished.

'Shall we walk?' He gestured to the wide path which led into the park, and the self-assured expression on his face was almost too much.

'It's what I came here for.' She didn't wait to see if he was following, but moments later she knew he'd fallen into step beside her; even if she hadn't glanced at him, she would have known. The tingle which shimmied down her spine told her he was close. It also warned her that her body hadn't forgotten his yet.

'The engagement feature has done all it

was expected to—and more.' He dropped the words between her, but she stopped, not able to concentrate on walking and thinking of that photo. The one where she'd looked so happy, so in love. Had he noticed that too?

'So my job is done?' She looked up at him, his expression serious as she studied his face, looking for any hint that he felt something for her. He looked down into her eyes, the grey of his stone-like. Was that what he'd come here to say? That her job was done and their fake engagement was now over?

She didn't want to hear that. She didn't know if she could say goodbye to the man she loved, but she was far too proud to tell him or even hint at deeper feelings. She thought again of the love letter, of those words written in beautiful flowing handwriting, from one lover to another. It was all she'd ever wanted—to be loved like that.

As Liev's expression hardened, she knew that would never be possible. Everything about him was cold and severe. His challenging stance as they stood in the sunshine of the afternoon, the sounds of the park all around them, told her all she needed to know. He didn't want her for anything other than forging his way into society. Now that had been achieved, she was surplus to requirements.

'It is, yes.' His lips set in a firm line and she could see his jaw clenching. Whatever had come to life between them on the island was now gone. If she was honest with herself, she'd accepted it had died the minute a new day had dawned.

Liev watched Bianca nod as they stood there, couples and families moving around them, seemingly oblivious to the tension which stretched almost to breaking point between them. She barely had any make-up on. Her hair, normally sleekly styled, was loose around her face. She looked so vulnerable, so emotionally exposed, it stabbed at him, plunging into his conscience and his heart. He'd done this to her; he was responsible for breaking her, for taking a fiery and passionate woman and destroying her.

He savagely pushed that guilt aside. She was the one who'd sold her body, bargained with her virginity, just to get a bracelet. He would never have asked that of her, never have taken it, had he known. She was as driven to achieve her goal as he was. But what exactly was that goal? Why was the bracelet *that* important?

He'd been seeking revenge for his parents, for his lost childhood. She should have just been an instrument to gain access to the man who'd offered his father that dubious deal, but instead he'd hurt her in the worst possible way, forced her to do something she'd never have done if it hadn't been the only way.

'Bianca,' he began, but she swiftly cut him off.

'Don't, Liev.'

'Don't what?' Guilt cut through him as he saw the pain and mistrust in her eyes. It hurt that he'd done that to her. It hurt because she'd unlocked something deep within him he'd thought crushed by the hand life had dealt him, something he wanted, although he'd never thought he would.

He couldn't comprehend it. He cared for Bianca, in a way he thought he'd never care for another person again. But Bianca, like Dario, had only ever been a means to an end. They didn't have any kind of future together.

'Don't say you are sorry. Not when using me so spectacularly was always part of the plan.' The pain in her voice was so clear, so sharp, it almost cut him.

He wanted to tell her that making love to her had never been part of his plan. He hadn't intended to kiss her—other than publicly for the sake of their fake engagement. But he could see it in her eyes, in the dark accusation within their depths. She thought he'd used her in the worst possible way, just to advance his name. How could he ever tell her it was so much more?

'I *am* sorry, Bianca, because I care for you.' The effort of keeping his voice firm and steady made it sound unnaturally harsh.

She looked suspiciously at him. 'That's a lie. If you cared you wouldn't have left it all week to come and tell me. You'd have told me before we left my grandfather's home, before we left your island villa. You would never have let me believe I'd become nothing more than just another notch on your bedpost.'

'You could never be that.' He took hold of her arms and looked into her face, wanting to kiss away the pain. This was killing him as much as it was her. 'I didn't come and see you because I couldn't face acknowledging what had happened between us. That night should not have happened. Not like that.'

That much was true. He'd put everything aside, forgotten everything, just to be with her, just to explore the passion and desire which had simmered since that day at the auction.

He'd wanted her in a way he'd wanted no other woman, beguiled by her innocence, driven by desire.

Their recent time together had shown him who he could have been and who she really was. It had made him yearn for things he'd thought off-limits to an undeserving man such as him, and whatever it was, it had to end. Right here. Right now.

He couldn't allow it to deter him from his graveside promise. He would avenge his parents, even if it meant turning his back on the only woman to have ever made him feel emotion.

'I came to give you this.' He held out the box which contained the bracelet, watched as her dark eyes glanced down at it, then back at him. He could see she wanted to take it and run. He put it back inside his jacket pocket, the agony of knowing it was all she wanted too painful.

'Does that mean our engagement is over?' She turned and walked on, leaving him no option but to fall into step beside her again.

He should say yes, but something held him back. She might have achieved an exclusive which had portrayed the ultimate love story to the world, opening the doors to society he'd led her to believe he'd wanted opening, but there was still one more thing he had to know.

'The deal will be completed once I hand over the bracelet, but before I do…' He paused and she glanced up at him.

'What, Liev?' The resigned tiredness in her voice tugged at his heart, finally awakened by that one night they'd put aside everything and truly loved one another. Or so he'd thought.

She walked to a bench and sat down, crossing her legs and twisting round to face him slightly. Her beautiful dark eyes urged him to talk even though she didn't say a word, and he would never forget how they'd looked as he'd made her his—only his. But he couldn't let such thoughts sway him; he couldn't fall for her charms and innocence, not when they were used against him as a weapon, one more powerful than anything he'd ever battled with before.

'I want to know exactly why the bracelet is so important.'

Bianca's heart went into free fall as she looked at Liev standing before her—alone. People milled around him but he was still very much alone. She wanted to go to him and tell him the bracelet had ceased to have any importance the moment he'd kissed her on the beach. That as he'd taken her to his bed and claimed her as his, binding her to him for ever, it had paled into total insignificance. No amount of glittering jewels was more important than love, and somehow she knew her grandfather would share that thought.

What would Liev say if she admitted that? Would he laugh at her? Would he believe her if she declared her love for him? If his reaction to her virginity was anything to go by, he would never believe a word she said again.

'It's complicated.' She focused her attention on the fountain as it stood majestically rising into the blue summer sky. Even the lily in the angel's hand, representing purity, mocked her for what he thought she'd done, giving her virginity for the bracelet. Would he ever believe her if she told him it wasn't true?

He came and sat next to her, and whilst she was rigidly perched on the edge of it, he leant back and stretched his arm out along the back of the bench. 'I'm listening.'

She closed her eyes and knew she would have to tell him everything if she stood any chance of him ever believing that she loved him. She'd come this far, fallen for the worst man possible, but after years of waiting, could she really turn her back on her love for him?

'As you know, my grandfather is ill—terminally ill.' She paused. Saying it aloud made it seem more real. Until now it had just been a fact in her head. 'Once, he'd owned that bracelet. I have no idea if he bought it for a lover or if it is a family heirloom, but when he arrived in New York in 1942, he had nothing to live off but a few pieces of jewellery. They must have meant something to him because he has asked for them, wanting to see them one last time.'

She moved slightly on the bench and turned to face Liev. He looked relaxed and not at all affected by her words, but the hand which rested on his thigh was clenched into a tight fist.

'And you bartered yourself, your virginity, for that?' The shock in his voice brought heated colour to her cheeks. Did he have to make it sound so bad, so cold and calculated?

She dropped her gaze and looked at her hands. Shamefully she would have to admit he was right, although it hadn't been like that at all. That night nothing else had mattered, only the man she'd loved, the man she'd waited for.

Unfortunately, he hadn't seen it that way. If she told him the truth, that she'd given him her virginity because she loved him, he would no doubt push her further away. He didn't let emotions rule that cold heart of his. She was fighting a lost cause. As far as he was concerned, she'd bartered with her body for a piece of jewellery. So what did that make her in his eyes? As callous and unfeeling as him?

She drew in a ragged breath and locked her heart away, smothered her emotions and looked directly into his eyes. 'I did and now I want what you promised me.'

Liev pulled the old box back out of his pocket and held it as he looked at her. His first impressions of Bianca had been right. She'd fooled him, tricked him. Made him believe he was special, that maybe if things had been different they could have had a future. She had been as callous and calculating as he'd been. No, worse. She'd brought emotions into their deal.

'I hope this makes your grandfather very happy, Bianca—and that it was worth it for you.'

She took the box from him, her fingers brushing against his, sending a fizz of electric awareness instantly through him. Inwardly he cursed. It didn't matter what she'd done, that she'd played on his past and exploited her innocence, leading him to do the one thing that he should never have done—take her virginity. None of that mattered. He still wanted her. And worse—what he felt for her went deeper, but he couldn't acknowledge that now.

'It was. One day, Liev, you, too, will do absolutely anything for love.' Her dark eyes were so hard, so fiercely full of contempt for him, that for a moment he was agonisingly jealous of her grandfather, for having all her love. There wasn't anything left. Not even the smallest space in her heart.

Once again he leapt to the defence of his emotions, the way he felt about her, desperate not to show the tiniest bit of compassion for her.

'Then we are both even.'

'Even?'

'Do you really imagine all I wanted was acceptance into New York society?' The wound she'd opened that night in his bed gaped wider and all he wanted was for her to hurt too.

She looked at him as if suddenly seeing a new person, disbelief and shock all over her pretty face.

'No, Bianca, I wanted to avenge the needless deaths of my parents and the destruction of my father's company—by ICE. Now, thanks to you, I have everything I need to bring your brother's company to its knees.'

He saw the moment realisation dawned, saw how she remembered telling him all he needed to know about Dario's launch while she was distracted by thoughts of her grandfather at the family home. She knew she'd told him everything.

'You truly are despicable.' She slid away from him on the bench, the bracelet box clutched ever tighter in her hands. 'You disgust me.'

'Maybe we are not so different after all, Bianca.' He moved towards her, seeing the anger glitter in her eyes. 'You wanted the bracelet for your grandfather and I want to bring down ICE. I want to avenge my father and put right the wrongs of the past, and, like you, I will do anything to achieve that.'

'No.' She shook her head in denial, a frown furrowing her brow. 'No. You've got it all wrong.'

'My father's company was destroyed, taken apart piece by piece by ICE, which ultimately destroyed him. My mother went to an early grave and my father soon followed, leaving me on the streets and very much alone. Have you any idea what it is like to be a twelve-year-old boy stealing stale bread just to exist? Have you any idea what it's like to be thrown in prison or to want revenge so badly you are driven by it day after day?'

She shook her head, her neat brows pulled together in such a way that he almost believed she could really feel all he was telling her. Was that sympathy or pity in her eyes? 'No, Liev, you are wrong.'

'I don't think I've got anything wrong, Bianca.' He could barely keep the snarl from his voice. His heart hammered so loudly with the injustice and anticipation of being so close to his lifelong ambition.

'Dario isn't responsible. You can't use that against him.' The pleading of her voice wasn't going to affect him; it wasn't going to sway him from his plans. He wouldn't allow her to distract him again.

'Granted, he didn't own ICE. He made a big show of putting right the company's past wrongs when he took over, but that was all lies, Bianca. A cover-up to inflate the share prices. He's no better than the man who did own ICE—and now they will pay.'

Liev stood, icy cold flowing through him despite the August sunshine. There was nothing more for him here. He was done with Bianca, done with emotions.

'Don't do this, Liev. Don't destroy my brother. For me, please reconsider.' She reached for him, but he moved back. If she touched him, sent that spark of desire through him, he wouldn't be able to remain strong.

'It's too late for that.' He clenched his teeth hard together. Did she have to play that card? Did she have to nudge his conscience and dig at his heart? He'd never come close to loving a woman, not until he'd met Bianca Di Sione.

'Please, Liev.'

Fool, he inwardly berated himself. 'You mean nothing to me. Dario is nothing, and if I don't do this for my father, then I, too, am nothing.'

Silently she stood up, her eyes locking with his, and he watched as she pulled the ring, his engagement ring, from her finger and held it out to him. He took it, feeling the warmth of her skin lingering on the gold band. No, he wouldn't be distracted.

'Go to Dario.' Her words were full of fury and disgust. Full of hatred for him. He could sense it with every bone in his body. 'Tell him what you know and find out what really happened.'

'Believe me, Bianca, I have every intention of doing exactly that.' He glared at her, matching her anger and denying he had any other emotion towards her.

'Go. Bring down his company, get your damn revenge. I don't care, Liev. Just leave me out of it.' She stepped back as if he was the devil himself, uncaring of the attention she was attracting from passers-by.

He walked calmly to her, every step making it more final. They were over before they'd even begun. 'I will and I intend to be every bit as calculating as you were.'

'I hate you.' Her voice had lowered and her eyes were narrow with hardness. 'And to think that I… Oh, just go. I never want to see you again—ever.'

He didn't wait to hear any more. Instead he turned and strode back through the park. She hated him and never wanted to see him again. She'd got what she wanted and now it was time to get what he wanted. The past two months had been about revenge, not the woman who had slipped beneath his defences, and the only way to remind himself of that was to exact that revenge.

CHAPTER TWELVE

FOR THE REST of the weekend, Bianca had tortured herself, worrying over Dario and what Liev intended to do. She'd expected to hear from Dario, but nothing other than the usual emails regarding the launch. Finally she'd broken under the pressure and had called him, explaining she'd given away all the necessary information to ruin him.

She'd explained about the bracelet and how Liev had bid against her in order to use it as blackmail. She had been so shocked when Dario had told her he, too, had just been given a task of locating a Lost Mistress that she confessed absolutely everything, even telling her brother she'd fallen in love with the man who was planning his downfall.

That man's silence had screamed at her all week, fraying her nerves. What was he up to? In just one hour ICE was about to launch its latest product, the one she'd stupidly told Liev all about, and all she could think of now was his warning that he wanted to bring ICE down and Dario with it.

He'd used her. Blackmailed her. But still she remembered his kisses. The night they'd made love. What was the matter with her?

The conference room was filling up fast. The press had already taken up their positions as Bianca slipped in the door at the side of the room to give everything one final check. Dario joined her, filled with excitement.

'You've done a great job, Bianca.' Her brother's voice was full of praise. Praise she didn't deserve.

'That's not true and you know it.'

'We all make mistakes. Don't worry—I've got your back on this one. It's all sorted.'

She turned to look at her brother. 'What do you mean?'

He placed his hands on her shoulders, forcing her to look up at him, and then smiled. 'It's sorted. Stop stressing and concentrate on your job.'

'But...' Before she could say any more, Dario had left. The room was filling more rapidly now and she watched everyone. Then her world stopped turning. Her heart stopped beating and she wasn't sure she could even breathe.

Liev.

She closed her eyes in resignation of all that was surely about to happen. Liev Dragunov wanted revenge and he was here to get exactly that. Her first instinct was to warn Dario, but he was busy with final preparations.

She had no choice. She had to confront Liev—now—before he publicly created a scene.

Trying to gather her shattered nerves, she strode over to him. Instantly the air became full of tension and the way he dominated everything around him unnerved her further. The dark suit he wore hugged his body and that image she'd stored away, of him standing in the sea, sunlight defining every muscle, filled her mind. What was the matter with her? The expression on his face was unreadable as she looked directly into his eyes.

'We need to talk, but not here.' Bianca walked away, hoping Liev would follow. She glanced back to see that he was, and that inscrutable expression didn't give her any hope that he'd changed his mind about revenge.

She went through the side doors, into the quietness of the corridor, and headed to the office she and Dario were using. Anywhere was better than having this conversation in public. Once inside the room, she stood behind the desk and turned to face him as he came in and shut the door.

His icy grey eyes met hers. 'I've seen Dario.'

Straight for the jugular, then. No niceties. But what had she expected—or more to the point, what had she hoped for?

'And?' She wasn't going to be drawn into giving anything else away. Not again.

He crossed the room and came to stand in front of her, only the polished surface of her desk between them. She could see the slate grey of his eyes glittering with anger. The firm set of his lips was so severe she wondered how she could ever have been seduced by his kiss. *Because you wanted him. Because you loved him.* The answers rushed at her and she stood a little taller in defence against what he was going to say.

'You were right.' His accent was harsher than she'd ever heard it, as if admitting such a thing was too difficult. The relief which rushed through her was immense, but it was soon hotly followed by panic.

'About what?' She didn't want to assume anything. Despite Liev's threat, ICE's share prices had risen steadily. Did this mean he still had his trump card to play? Was that why he was here?

He calmly sat down, as if they were having a friendly chat, but the darkening of his eyes urged caution. Her attention was snagged as he stretched out his strong legs, looking powerful and relaxed, like a panther luring its prey in for the kill—and she had no intention of being his prey.

'Dario had tried to put those dubious dealings right. I saw the evidence for myself.' He watched her intently as she sat down and a zip of something travelled down her spine. Fear? Yes, that was it. How had he managed to obtain such information? She only knew what Dario had told her in the past; she'd never seen any evidence.

'He wouldn't just show you something like that.' Why hadn't Dario told her about this? He knew how worried she was, how guilty she felt. 'When did this happen?'

'Monday.' The word slid through the air at her and she looked at him, and for a moment she thought she saw a hint of a smile on his lips. Damn him. Did it amuse him to torment her like this?

Why hadn't Dario said anything to her? It

must have been some showdown, but with the share prices rising, it was one Liev had obviously lost. Distractedly she dragged her fingers through her hair and looked at the few papers on her desk, as if they could give her all the answers she sought. Anything not to look into that handsome face.

'You obviously didn't carry out your planned revenge, so what is it you want now, Liev?' She returned her attention to his face and saw the lift of his brows and again that fleeting hint of a smile. What was he up to? Just as the first time she'd met him, she didn't trust him one bit.

He stood up and walked around the desk, to stand next to it and look out of the tall window at the skyscrapers of New York. His bold audacity at helping himself to such a view jarred on her already jangling nerves. She stood up, too, not happy to sit whilst he all but loomed so close.

'Liev,' she snapped, hardly able to contain the apprehension inside her. 'What do you want this time?'

'This time?' He turned to face her and to her horror took a step closer, then another, until she could breathe in the scent of his aftershave, which only made her more worried as somewhere deep inside her the flicker of hot passion they'd shared stirred once more. She couldn't allow him to dominate her, to drag her back to the night she'd loved with her heart and her body.

'Yes, this time.' Her terse words rushed out. 'The last time you wanted something, it was to blackmail me in order to destroy my brother's company. Not that you told me that—no, you lied and cheated your way into my...'

She stopped, inwardly cursing herself. She'd almost given herself away, almost told him he'd cheated his way into her heart. Just as she'd almost told him she loved him whilst they'd been in Central Park last weekend. Thank goodness she'd stopped herself each time. He could never know he had that power over her.

'Into your what, Bianca?' He took another step closer and she drew in a breath, determined not to step back, not to be intimidated by him, but even more determined he should never know the truth.

'My family, my social circle. You told me you wanted acceptance and I tried to give you that, even though it was just a cover for the destructive revenge you planned.'

'I did want acceptance, but things changed.'

He remained so close she could hardly think straight.

So he still wanted revenge. 'If you have all you want, I think you should go.'

She turned away from him, looking out over the city as it shimmered in the heat of the afternoon. She didn't need this conversation now, not when the launch was about to happen.

'I'm not leaving, Bianca, not yet. Not when I don't have everything I want.'

Her fingers curled tightly into the palms of her hands, her nails digging in painfully, focusing her mind. She whirled round to face him, her chin lifted defiantly. She would put an end to this right now.

'What do you want, Liev?'

'You.'

Liev watched Bianca's eyes widen in shock and outrage, but this was no longer a time for dancing around issues and giving mixed messages. He had to tell her exactly what he wanted, exactly why he was here. The rest was up to her. He was totally at her mercy.

'How dare you?' She flung the accusation at him, disbelief in her eyes, on her beautiful face and in every move she made. Then she stepped back, watching him suspiciously as she did so.

'Don't deny it, Bianca. You want me as much as I want you.' He moved towards her, but stopped when alarm entered her eyes. He had no wish to frighten her, not when everything he'd done this week had been done to avoid hurting her in any way.

'All I want is for you to leave—right now.' She squared up to him, just as she had done after he'd bought the bracelet, outbidding her and infuriating her.

If he was honest with himself, he'd fallen in love with her right then, but he just hadn't recognised it as love. To him it had been the first stirrings of desire, but he'd pushed that aside in his quest for revenge. At least until he'd taken her to the island villa. It had been as they'd made love, abandoning everything in their past to enjoy that night, that he'd accepted he was in love with her, but that had been instantly quashed when she'd admitted to using her virginity just to get the bracelet. Instead he'd despised her. He'd thought she was as callous as he believed her brother to be.

'That's not the impression you gave to Dario.' Now he really had her attention.

'No.' She shook her head. 'He wouldn't have told you.'

'What? That you'd fallen in love with your blackmailer?'

She gasped and for a moment he thought she was going to crumple to the floor in shock. Her blue eyes were so wide, their colour so vivid. Then she dragged in a deep breath and fixed a furious expression to her face. 'He had no right to tell any such thing.'

'So, it's true?'

'No.' Her voice rose and he knew she was lying, deceiving herself as well as him. All he had to do now was convince her that he loved her, that because of that love he'd changed all the plans for revenge. 'I despise you. How can I ever love a man who wants to do nothing but destroy my brother and me in the process?'

'How could you make love to a man, give up your virginity, if you didn't love him?' She paled as his words found their mark and he felt sorry for her, felt her pain and confusion, and wanted nothing more than to hold her, to kiss away that pain, caress away that confusion.

'I did it for the bracelet, for my grandfather.' She fiddled nervously with the simple gold locket around her neck and bit down on her bottom lip as she waited for his response.

'I know,' he said softly, and he moved towards her. 'You have no idea how much it hurts me to think that I put you in that position.'

'You blackmailed me, Liev, blackmailed me in order to ruin my brother. I can never forgive you for that—ever.'

The door opened and one of Dario's staff came in. 'Sorry. Ten minutes until we go live.'

'Thank you.' Bianca was visibly unnerved and her eyes met his, the questions in them clear. He'd do anything to take away her pain, to answer those questions, but in the light of what she'd just told him, he knew it might never happen.

'Excuse me. I have to go.'

Panic sluiced through him. She had to know what he'd done in an attempt to mend the hurt he'd caused. He had to make her understand he loved her, but from the sound of that last comment, his time was very limited.

She looked at him. 'I have work to do, Liev. I'd like you to leave.'

'Not yet, you don't. I need to explain.' He stood so close to her he could smell her fragrance and he remembered how she felt in his arms. He had to fight for that.

'There's nothing to explain. You deceived me, blackmailed me and now you plan to destroy all that my brother has worked to achieve. How can there be anything to add to that?'

There was so much more to add, like the deal he'd struck with Dario after the heated argument which had revealed the truth of the situation. A deal that meant he could put right the past in a businesslike way and not hurt anyone in the process. He had, of course, faced Dario's wrath over hurting his sister and it was then that her confession to her brother had unintentionally come out, but Dario must have got it wrong. She didn't have feelings for him. From the contempt on her face, it was obvious she had no wish to see him at all.

'I didn't use anything you told me, Bianca— not to anyone but Dario.' He'd never felt this out of depth before, this adrift in a sea of emotions he couldn't control.

'But what is to stop you leaving here right now and doing just that?'

'There is only one thing that can stop me,' he said, his voice gravelly and thick with emotion. 'You.'

She shook her head. 'It's too late, Liev, too much has happened, and besides, I don't believe you and certainly don't trust you. You could leave here now and leak all you know, just moments before the launch, to the waiting press and achieve the destruction you so obviously crave.'

'Why would I destroy a company I'm now a shareholder in?'

CHAPTER THIRTEEN

HE WAS A SHAREHOLDER? As the sounds of the launch filtered into the office, Bianca's mind reeled. What had he done? He'd been so angry when he'd left the park, so hell-bent on getting revenge, but this was the last thing she expected to hear.

Why had he waited until now to say anything? Why moments before the launch? What was he up to? The need to warn Dario rushed over her again and she realised sending Liev away would only give him the perfect opportunity for taking his revenge at the worst possible moment.

'What did you do, Liev?' She asked the question, hating the trepidation in her voice. None of what he was saying made any sense, and why was it all connected to her?

'I did exactly what you told me to do. I went to see Dario. I went with the intention of telling him I knew all about his latest product, that I would leak it all to the media as payment for what ICE had done to my family. I wanted revenge and Dario was the way to get to the man who'd been responsible for destroying so many companies.'

She saw his jaw clench as he finished speaking, as if he was trying to bite down the anger he felt. Nothing made sense. Had he blackmailed Dario too? But her brother would never take that. Would he?

'What did Dario say?' Her voice was more of a cracked whisper as she hardly dared to ask. Liev must have seen Dario after she'd called him; otherwise her brother would have said something when she'd called to confess what she'd done. Thank goodness she'd finally plucked up the courage to tell him. At least he would have been forewarned. Then she recalled her brother's words. *I've got it covered.* What had he meant?

Liev crossed back to the window, looking far too much in control of himself and the discussion. How did he always manage to turn everything to his advantage? He'd even turned a prison sentence into something beneficial to him.

'Dario listened to all I had to say, some-

thing I did not expect. Then he picked up a
file, one he had ready after your warning call.
He showed the various correspondences that
had been made to my father or his beneficiary.
As you know from your research on me, I'd
purposefully lived under the radar. The letters
never reached me.'

'And that's why you didn't leak the information you so cruelly duped out of me?' Bianca's mind was racing to keep up with these
new events. Surely Dario would have called
her, told her what had happened.

'In part, but I couldn't have gone through
with it, Bianca.'

He turned those slate grey eyes on her and
her heart flipped, sending a dart of annoyance through her. She shouldn't feel anything
for this mercenary man. 'So our sham of an
engagement has been wasted? The past two
months have been for nothing?'

'Hell, Bianca, can't you see? I couldn't go
through with it because it would hurt *you*.'

She looked at him, suspicion filling her
mind, her heart. What was he trying to do
now? Make her think he actually had feelings
for her? That he felt guilty for what he'd done?

'You are just saying that because it's all gone
wrong. All you want is to justify blackmailing

me and keeping an old man from something he treasured.'

'I'm saying it because…' He paused and she looked at him warily. 'Because I love you, Bianca.'

A heavy silence settled between them and she blinked in shock. Had she heard right? Had he said the words that deep down she'd wanted to hear—and from him?

'You love me?' The question slipped from her lips in a silky whisper and she saw for the first time the anxiety in those grey eyes as he watched her, intense expectation on his handsome face.

This was almost too much. The man who had stolen her heart was confessing his love for her. Hope rushed through her. She blushed and she lowered her gaze beneath his fierce scrutiny. But how could the blackmailer become a lover? Was it possible?

'Yes, Bianca, I love you. Ever since my parents died, I've shut out sentiments I considered to be weakening. After one disastrous affair, I focused my energy on avenging the destruction of my father's business and ultimately life as I knew it.'

He paused again and she walked towards him, still unsure of what was really happening, but unable to resist the pull of attraction, the flare of hope which urged her to take a chance. He looked into her eyes as she stood before him and then slowly reached out and took her hand in his and drew her closer. She couldn't speak, couldn't break the heady spell that had filled her office.

'You've changed all that. You brought light back into my life. You made me feel real, whole. Bianca, you *are* my life.'

'But what about ICE?' She had to ask. She couldn't ignore the launch that was probably happening right now.

Liev looked down into Bianca's face, saw the worry and confusion swirling in her eyes and longed to kiss her, to prove what he felt was real. But he had more explaining to do yet.

'Dario was understandably angry.' That was an understatement. He'd been furious, but as he'd given vent to his anger, not over the fact that Liev had wanted to ruin the business as a means of revenge, but the fact that he'd used Bianca so appallingly, Dario had let slip one important bit of information.

How could you use Bianca so cruelly? Don't you know she loves you? Dario's words had sliced through the angry atmosphere, shattering all his plans for revenge as if they were made of the finest crystal and had just been hit with a rod of iron. He'd known then that the revenge he'd wanted for years could never be taken. Not when the woman who'd stolen his heart loved him, despite her claims of hate the day he'd given her the bracelet and she'd returned the ring.

'But you told him—about your father's business?' She looked up at him, all wide-eyed and innocent, and again the urge to press her to him and kiss her forged forward.

'That was easily sorted, once he showed me the file. What he wasn't so easily placated over was the way I'd treated you—and rightly so.' He brushed his fingertips over her face, watched as her eyelashes fluttered briefly closed.

'I knew all along that would be a problem when we ended our engagement. I just hoped none of my brothers or sisters would find out about the deal I'd struck for the bracelet.' Her earnest words cut him deeply. How could he have been so callous? She hadn't deserved any of that. 'What did he say?'

Most of what Dario had said he couldn't repeat, but one sentence had kept playing over and over in his mind, until he knew he had to come and see her, had to risk everything. *Don't you know she loves you?*

'That I'd hurt you, treated you badly, didn't deserve you. The usual brotherly type of things.' He tried to inject lightness into his voice, but as his last words rushed out, he failed. 'And he was right.'

'No, no, don't say that.' The husky whisper forced his eyes closed, and when he looked at her again she was smiling up at him. 'That's what brothers do—and offer you a deal so that you don't have to break my heart all over again.'

'All over again? When did I first break your heart?'

'After that night on the island.' She blushed and lowered her lashes, and he lifted her chin so she had to look at him. He wanted to see the reality of her love in her eyes. 'You looked so disgusted with me.'

He let a harsh Russian curse slip out, realising how it must have looked to her. She'd been at her most vulnerable then and he'd hurt her at the worst possible time. 'I was disgusted with myself for pushing you into that situation.'

She reached up and pressed her lips against his briefly. 'None of that matters now, Liev, and I wouldn't have changed that night for anything. It was perfect.'

Before she could say anything else, he kissed her, her response firing the need within him, and he had to force himself to stop. He loved her, and as he'd looked into her eyes, he'd seen her love reflected back at him.

Bianca wanted to keep kissing him, to savour every last minute of the kiss. She loved him. He'd changed her and changed the way she viewed men, albeit in an unorthodox way, but he had and she meant what she'd said. That night they'd spent on his island together was special and she couldn't ever forget it, wish it undone, for anything. That night she had loved him—truly loved him.

Her grandfather had known that she'd fallen deeply in love with Liev; she was convinced of that now. Thankfully she didn't think he knew that Liev had blackmailed her, but he had known she loved him and was holding back, denying herself love. 'Do you know what my grandfather said just before we left?'

She felt Liev's arms tense around her and his eyes narrowed slightly in suspicion. 'What did he say?'

'He told me that whatever I did, I shouldn't waste a chance of love if it comes along.' She smiled at him, her heart beating hard with love for him. 'And I don't intend to waste it, Liev.'

He closed his eyes in relief, his arms losing their tension, but not lessening their hold on her. 'Bianca, how can I ever make it up to you, put right all the wrong I've done?'

'Love me.'

'There was a moment in the park last week when I wanted to tell you I loved you...that I didn't care about revenge, that all I cared about was you. Do you remember telling me I would one day do anything for love?'

'Yes,' she whispered, remembering those exact words.

'I was almost blinded with jealousy because of the love you had for your grandfather.'

'It wasn't my grandfather I was referring to—or the bracelet. It was you and that night at the villa.'

Liev didn't answer her, at least not with words. Instead he claimed her lips, pulling her so hard against him that she could hardly breathe, but it was exactly where she wanted to be. His hands caressed her and beneath the business suit she wore her body burst into flames.

'There is only one thing left to do.' He held her away from him to look into her eyes, his full of desire matching that which raced through her. He stepped back and pulled the ring from his pocket, holding it between his fingers so it glinted beneath the lights. 'You can choose a different ring if you want, but, Bianca Di Sione, will you do me the great honour of becoming my wife? My real wife.'

'Yes,' she whispered. This was the happy ending she'd secretly longed for all her life, since reading that letter, the one so full of love. 'Yes, Liev, I will and I don't want a different ring—this one is just perfect.'

He kissed her more deeply than he'd ever kissed her and eventually his lips left hers, leaving her so breathless she could hardly utter a word. 'Bianca Di Sione, I love you so very much. You have made my life complete.'

* * * * *

If you enjoyed this book,
look out for the next instalment of
THE BILLIONAIRE'S LEGACY:
THE RETURN OF THE DI SIONE WIFE
by Caitlin Crews.
Coming next month.

LARGER-PRINT BOOKS!

GET 2 FREE LARGER-PRINT NOVELS PLUS
2 FREE GIFTS!

HARLEQUIN

Romance

From the Heart, For the Heart

LARGER-PRINT BOOKS!
GET 2 FREE LARGER-PRINT NOVELS PLUS
2 FREE GIFTS!

HARLEQUIN

super romance

More Story...More Romance

YES! Please send me 2 FREE LARGER-PRINT Harlequin® Superromance® novels and my 2 FREE gifts (gifts are worth about $10). After receiving them, if I don't wish to receive any more books, I can return the shipping statement marked "cancel." If I don't cancel, I will receive 4 brand-new novels every month and be billed just $5.94 per book in the U.S. or $6.24 per book in Canada. That's a savings of at least 12% off the cover price! It's quite a bargain! Shipping and handling is just 50¢ per book in the U.S. or 75¢ per book in Canada.* I understand that accepting the 2 free books and gifts places me under no obligation to buy anything. I can always return a shipment and cancel at any time. Even if I never buy another book, the two free books and gifts are mine to keep forever.

132/332 HDN GHVC

Name _____ (PLEASE PRINT)

Address _____ Apt. #

City _____ State/Prov. _____ Zip/Postal Code

Signature (if under 18, a parent or guardian must sign)

Mail to the **Reader Service:**
IN U.S.A.: P.O. Box 1867, Buffalo, NY 14240-1867
IN CANADA: P.O. Box 609, Fort Erie, Ontario L2A 5X3

Want to try two free books from another line?
Call 1-800-873-8635 today or visit www.ReaderService.com.

* Terms and prices subject to change without notice. Prices do not include applicable taxes. Sales tax applicable in N.Y. Canadian residents will be charged applicable taxes. Offer not valid in Quebec. This offer is limited to one order per household. Not valid for current subscribers to Harlequin Superromance Larger-Print books. All orders subject to credit approval. Credit or debit balances in a customer's account(s) may be offset by any other outstanding balance owed by or to the customer. Please allow 4 to 6 weeks for delivery. Offer available while quantities last.

Your Privacy—The Reader Service is committed to protecting your privacy. Our Privacy Policy is available online at www.ReaderService.com or upon request from the Reader Service.

We make a portion of our mailing list available to reputable third parties that offer products we believe may interest you. If you prefer that we not exchange your name with third parties, or if you wish to clarify or modify your communication preferences, please visit us at www.ReaderService.com/consumerchoice or write to us at Reader Service Preference Service, P.O. Box 9062, Buffalo, NY 14240-9062. Include your complete name and address.

HSRLP15

LARGER-PRINT BOOKS!
GET 2 FREE LARGER-PRINT NOVELS PLUS
2 FREE GIFTS!

HARLEQUIN®

INTRIGUE
BREATHTAKING ROMANTIC SUSPENSE

YES! Please send me 2 FREE LARGER-PRINT Harlequin® Intrigue novels and my 2 FREE gifts (gifts are worth about $10). After receiving them, if I don't wish to receive any more books, I can return the shipping statement marked "cancel." If I don't cancel, I will receive 6 brand-new novels every month and be billed just $5.49 per book in the U.S. or $6.24 per book in Canada. That's a saving of at least 11% off the cover price! It's quite a bargain! Shipping and handling is just 50¢ per book in the U.S. and 75¢ per book in Canada.* I understand that accepting the 2 free books and gifts places me under no obligation to buy anything. I can always return a shipment and cancel at any time. Even if I never buy another book, the two free books and gifts are mine to keep forever.

199/399 HDN GHWN

Name _____ (PLEASE PRINT)

Address _____ Apt. #

City _____ State/Prov. _____ Zip/Postal Code

Signature (if under 18, a parent or guardian must sign) _____

Mail to the Reader Service:
IN U.S.A.: P.O. Box 1867, Buffalo, NY 14240-1867
IN CANADA: P.O. Box 609, Fort Erie, Ontario L2A 5X3

**Are you a subscriber to Harlequin® Intrigue books
and want to receive the larger-print edition?
Call 1-800-873-8635 today or visit www.ReaderService.com.**

* Terms and prices subject to change without notice. Prices do not include applicable taxes. Sales tax applicable in N.Y. Canadian residents will be charged applicable taxes. Offer not valid in Quebec. This offer is limited to one order per household. Not valid for current subscribers to Harlequin Intrigue Larger-Print books. All orders subject to credit approval. Credit or debit balances in a customer's account(s) may be offset by any other outstanding balance owed by or to the customer. Please allow 4 to 6 weeks for delivery. Offer available while quantities last.

Your Privacy—The Reader Service is committed to protecting your privacy. Our Privacy Policy is available online at www.ReaderService.com or upon request from the Reader Service.

We make a portion of our mailing list available to reputable third parties that offer products we believe may interest you. If you prefer that we not exchange your name with third parties, or if you wish to clarify or modify your communication preferences, please visit us at www.ReaderService.com/consumerchoice or write to us at Reader Service Preference Service, P.O. Box 9062, Buffalo, NY 14240-9062. Include your complete name and address.

HILP15

WESTERN WP PROMISES

YES! Please send me **The Western Promises Collection** in Larger Print. This collection begins with 3 FREE books and 2 FREE gifts (gifts valued at approx. $14.00 retail) in the first shipment, along with the other first 4 books from the collection! If I do not cancel, I will receive 8 monthly shipments until I have the entire 51-book Western Promises collection. I will receive 2 or 3 FREE books in each shipment and I will pay just $4.99 US/ $5.89 CDN for each of the other four books in each shipment, plus $2.99 for shipping and handling per shipment. *If I decide to keep the entire collection, I'll have paid for only 32 books, because 19 books are FREE! I understand that accepting the 3 free books and gifts places me under no obligation to buy anything. I can always return a shipment and cancel at any time. My free books and gifts are mine to keep no matter what I decide.

272 HCN 3070 472 HCN 3070

Name _____ (PLEASE PRINT) _____

Address _____ Apt. # _____

City _____ State/Prov. _____ Zip/Postal Code _____

Signature (if under 18, a parent or guardian must sign)

Mail to the **Reader Service:**

IN U.S.A.: P.O. Box 1867, Buffalo, NY 14240-1867
IN CANADA: P.O. Box 609, Fort Erie, Ontario L2A 5X3

* Terms and prices subject to change without notice. Prices do not include applicable taxes. Sales tax applicable in N.Y. Canadian residents will be charged applicable taxes. This offer is limited to one order per household. All orders subject to approval. Credit or debit balances in a customer's account(s) may be offset by any other outstanding balance owed by or to the customer. Please allow 4 to 6 weeks for delivery. Offer available while quantities last. Offer not available to Quebec residents.

WPBPA16R